THE RUM JUNGLE HOTEL AND OTHER TRAVEL STORIES

Jonathan Evans

The Rum Jungle Hotel and Other Travel Stories
First published 2022 by LEED Ltd in conjunction with Tangent Books

LEED Ltd
25 Burghley Road Bristol BS6 5BL
07968637015
www.jonathanevanswriter.com
lloydevansltd@btinternet.com

Tangent Books
Unit 5.16 Paintworks, Bristol BS4 3EH
www.tangentbooks.co.uk

ISBN
978-0-9575016-8-3

Author: Jonathan Evans
Typesetting : Robert Atwood
Cover Design: Joe Burt from an initial idea by Harry Lloyd-Evans

A CIP record of this book is available at the British Library.

An' the dawn comes up like thunder
outer China 'crost the Bay.

Rudyard Kipling

CONTENTS

Introduction 7

PART ONE: **HITCHHIKING**

Chapter 1. The Diver 11
Chapter 2. Wrestlers 19
Chapter 3. Chickens 25
Chapter 4. Karlobag 78 31
Chapter 5. Joni Mitchell, the Prime Minister and the Exploding Freak 39
Chapter 6. Don 45
Chapter 7. The Fall 49

PART TWO: **AUSTRALIA**

Chapter 8. Shoot out at Seal Rocks 57
Chapter 9. Cauliflower 65
Chapter 10. Four Down 69
Chapter 11. Christmas at the Rum Jungle Hotel 71
Chapter 12. Herbie 77

PART THREE: **THE OVERLAND TRAIL**

Chapter 13. If Paradise Was Half as Nice 89
Chapter 14. The Path of Spirits 95
Chapter 15. Shroom 101
Chapter 16. The Atlanta Hotel 109
Chapter 17. The Man with the Golden Thing 115
Chapter 18. Wock 123
Chapter 19. The Meshad – Teheran Express 129
Chapter 20. Pierre 137

PART FOUR: **MEETINGS WITH REMARKABLE PEOPLE**

Chapter 21. Manila Diary 147
Chapter 22. My week with Hunter S Thompson 151
Chapter 23. Sheikh Rassoul and the Necklace of Tutankhamun 157
Chapter 24. Ramayana 161
Chapter 25. The Heart of Darkness 165
Chapter 26. An Evening with the Mad Strangler 169

POSTSCRIPT

Chapter 27. The Passenger 175

INTRODUCTION

"Maybe it meant something. Maybe not, in the long run, but no explanation, no mix of words or music or memories can touch that sense of knowing that you were there and alive in that corner of time and the world. Whatever it meant."
Hunter S. Thompson

It's been kind of quiet lately, so I've been going through a lot of junk in the house with the idea of finally getting rid of some things. I had to stop, though, when I came across a box full of old photographs. Most were of relatives and stuff, but one stood out, it was of a much younger and slimmer me hitchhiking on a dusty road in southern Spain. It was 1969 and, after a summer working in the bars of the Costa Brava, I was headed for Morocco where, after a series of unfortunate incidents which I won't go into just now, I ended up in hospital. Anyway, there I am, young, innocent and bound for glory and, as I looked at that photograph, memories of nearly forgotten names and places started trickling in.

I was so taken with the picture that I posted it on Facebook, and, after a while, other images started arriving. One was of me, again hitchhiking, in the Australian outback in the late 70s and then an old friend, Hilary, sent one of me standing outside the 'Cozy Corner Hubbly Bubbly Room' in Kathmandu.

Thinking about these photographs got me thinking about all the weird and wonderful people and places I've encountered over the years.

Some of the stories which follow are set in the late 1960s, a time before travel guides like Lonely Planet even existed, and most are set in the 70s and 80s, times when we could travel the world simply by putting our thumbs out, and letting the journey take us to wherever it wanted to go.

I hope you enjoy them.

PART ONE:
HITCHHIKING

Chapter 1:
The Diver

I'm more than a mile and a half from shore and treading water, desperately alone and very nervous. The wind is beginning to blow and there's a chop building. I get a mouthful of water and cough. Not for the first time, I'm beginning to feel as though I've really made a big mistake. The shore seems so far away and I know that even if I'm to head back now, my chances of making it are probably no better than fifty - fifty.

I had arrived in Folegandros by ferry from Santorini about four days earlier and was camping under the stars.

On about the fifth day a young guy made his way towards the beach. He was an Italian, Maurizio. He had a voice that sounded as though his larynx was lined with sandpaper, rasping but somehow appealing. He told me that he was from the south of Italy and was a medical student. As I got to know him better, he told me of his big passion.

"I hold the world record for diving without artificial aids."

He went on to explain that he could dive to about eighty metres. The only equipment he used was his nose clip and a pair of plastic goggles, very small, not the sort of thing you'd see a scuba diver wear but more like those you'd buy at your local swimming pool.

His physique was interesting. He was quite short, maybe five feet eight or nine. He had wiry black hair. His chest and upper torso were most unusual, the shape of a V, with very wide shoulders and a narrow waist. And, as for his legs, I can only describe them as the sort you'd normally see on a frog. Huge thigh muscles, enormous calves and feet like broad paddles. I guess you might say he had the ideal build for a swimmer.

Over a cup of coffee one morning, he casually told me that he could hold his breath for six minutes.

He looked at me. "After about three minutes, is no problem, your brain knows you no longer need to breathe." He explained that the brain is really sensitive to carbon dioxide and, as the level of carbon dioxide in the blood rises, part of the brain, the Medulla Oblongata, triggers a breathing reflex and this normally happens every couple of seconds. But, Maurizio told me, if you hold your beath long enough, the blood becomes so rich in carbon dioxide that the brain becomes confused, and it stops triggering the reflex. In other words, "If you hold your breath long enough you no longer feel the urge to breathe; this is the secret of diving deep."

I was intrigued by what Maurizio had told me, and I mentioned that I really wanted to go out and see for myself just how he did his diving.

"It is difficult here, the water is not deep. Maybe twenty metres. We have to go a long, long way from shore."

"How far?"

"I don't know, two, maybe three kilometres."

"Alright."

"If you like, maybe tomorrow, we try."

I thought for a second and then agreed. I wasn't a bad swimmer and Maurizio assured me that he would swim at a pace that I could keep up with.

The next morning was warm, as usual, and conditions were perfect. We had a big breakfast and decided to go.

We set off. Maurizio was swimming a lazy crawl and, even

though he was clearly taking it easy, he was soon leaving me behind, so he slowed, and I eventually caught up with him.

As we went further out, I noticed the sea beginning to change colour, from a light blue to a darker blue, then to an inky black.

I looked at my watch. We had been going for nearly an hour. Maurizio put his goggles on and looked down into the depths.

"We need to go further. Is only twenty-five metres here."

I wondered how much further we needed to go. I was beginning to feel a little worried. I was feeling the strain. This was certainly further than I'd ever swum in my life, and it was much tougher than I had anticipated.

Maurizio was reassuring, "It's easy, John, just swim on your back. If you're tired, rest your arms but keep kicking."

In this way we went for about another forty minutes.

The beach was just a smudge now, and sometimes as the waves came past, I'd lose sight of it all together.

Maurizio eventually decided to call a halt.

"Here. Here looks good, John. Maybe I try here."

"How long do you think you'll be?"

"Five minutes, maybe six."

"Okay."

He floated in the water upright and then began exhaling, blowing as much air as he could from his lungs, followed by huge gulping intakes of breath. I swear I could see the upper part of his body expand with each cycle of this process. He went through this ritual for maybe a minute and then, with a final inhalation, he waved and was gone.

I checked the time and watched him descend through the water. Slowly he spiralled downwards, moving with the least expenditure of energy possible. He became smaller and smaller. I looked at my watch. How long had he been gone? It seemed an age, but it was less than a minute.

As I looked down Maurizio eventually disappeared from sight into the depths.

Time seemed to drag. I was alone in the sea, maybe two miles from the shore. Some worrying thoughts came to me. What if Maurizio didn't return? Could I make it back by myself? I didn't know.

I looked at the watch, two minutes gone now. Looking down, there was not a sign, just darkness beneath me. I noticed that the wind had picked up and was beginning to chop the water. I was suddenly aware of feeling cold, and I began to shiver.

As the waves built, I got a mouthful of sea water and spluttered and nearly panicked. Almost immediately I got a dreadful cramp in my leg. This was serious. I knew that I could be in big trouble here.

I had to tell myself to keep calm. But where was Maurizio? The watch was moving slowly. It now registered three and a half minutes and still there was no sign.

In the distance I heard a low rumble and noticed that the sky had clouded over, and shadows were chasing over the surface of the sea. There was another rumble and I saw a flash of lightning and then a grey screen rushing towards me, rain. Now it began pouring down hard and still there was no Maurizio. It had now been more than five minutes and I began to get dreadfully concerned.

I lay face down in the water and, using my mask, started searching for him. The pain in my leg began to ease but I was really frightened. My stomach was in knots.

It was now nearly six minutes and I felt pretty sure that he was never coming back. I looked towards the shore and thought that it was time to cut my losses, but I took one last look and there, after almost seven minutes, I saw something circling slowly up towards the surface, coming up, up, up, closer and closer. Maurizio. He looked pained. Up he came and then broke the surface coughing and, as he did so, I noticed a smidgen of blood in his ear.

What I didn't know is that in the depths Maurizio had just had the battle of his life.

He was holding his head, gulping. He signalled to his ears –

"There's been a problem. Terrible, terrible. John. My ears ….. burst. Frio, frio, cold, so cold."

For the first time Maurizio was expressing urgency. He looked like an old man, and he clearly needed to get back. He was cold and I was worried because I knew that if Maurizio got into trouble, I probably wouldn't be able to help him.

We turned towards the shore. Fortunately, Maurizio was now doing breaststroke, the stroke he had used to descend. He seemed to be in a trance, but even so he was moving really quickly, and I had to work hard to try and keep up, but I couldn't.

After ten minutes I was way adrift and alone in the sea and again frightened because it was a long way, and my arms and legs were really aching. It had stopped raining now, but it was still blowing, and spray kept catching me. I was chafing under my arms and between my legs where the salt was rubbing. And then Maurizio came back.

He was shivering but flashed me a grimace.

"Come, we must get in."

That swim was probably the hardest thing I've ever done. I recall staggering onto the beach, my legs like rubber and, at first, I couldn't stand.

The first thing I noticed was Maurizio's chest. It was blue, the colour of damp clay and looked as though it was bruised.

We shivered for about an hour and built a camp fire to warm us up. My hands were like wrinkled prunes, and I had dried salt everywhere.

Eventually Maurizio shared with me what had happened. He was crunching some strong pain killers as he spoke.

"I am down deep, and I look at my watch. It says five minutes. So, it is time to come up; that's all I remember. Then I wake up. I know I have blacked out. My ears are in agony. I have burst my eardrums. The problem is that I lose all sense of balance and direction and I'm confused I do not know which way the surface is. I am at seventy metres."

"I have to keep calm and logical and let air out of my mouth. I know that air bubbles fly to the surface, so I release a stream from my mouth and swim after them. My brain says I am swimming sideways, but my logic tells me I am swimming towards the surface. All the way I am frightened, confused, but, as you can see, my logic saved my life. It was, how you say, a close thing."

In a remarkably short time Maurizio and I were up and about. We wandered the beach. It had been raining but now the sun was breaking through the clouds, and I saw a beauty in details that I had never noticed before. I felt truly alive. That night we ate enormously and drank even more than normal and yet I felt as though I could have carried on for ever. We came back down to our campsite at about three in the morning and at about seven o'clock Maurizio packed his gear to leave on the early boat to get attention for his damaged eardrums.

As I waved goodbye, I wondered whether I would ever see him again and in fact, for many years I didn't think that I would. However, one night, about twenty years later, I was in a bar, on another island, in another life and across the room I heard somebody in that unmistakable rasping voice asking for a beer.

I looked towards him. I wasn't sure about the appearance, older for sure, a bit rounder, a little less hair, but the voice was unmistakable.

I said "Maurizio, Is that you?"

He looked at me, a puzzled look in his eye.

"Do I know you?"

I said "Yes" and then, "Remember Folegandros?"

He looked at me again, a smile creased his face. He tweaked the lobe of his ear and said,

"John, shall we go for a swim tomorrow?"

Chapter 2:
Wrestlers

To paraphrase Emperor Hirohito, things were progressing, not necessarily to our advantage.

Somehow, in that summer of 1969, Chris and I had managed to get ourselves from the Ramblas, through the blinding sun to Sants railway station where we boarded a train for Blanes, the nearest stop to Lloret de Mar.

We arrived in scorching heat, our senses assailed by the smell of garlic and salt air. On the beach nothing moved apart from the haze above the baking tourists and a lone ice cream seller walking along sand that was as hot as coals crying out, "Ice cream aleka aleka aleka."

We sat, rucksacks at our backs, frying. After about five minutes Chris stood up, took off his shoes, ran down the beach and poured himself into the waves. He returned minutes later, his thick denim jeans and Bri-Nylon shirt dripping with water.

"Saves on washing powder," he said laconically.

That evening we went in search of somewhere to sleep. Although a *pension* was cheap – at about twenty-five pesetas, we were on a very tight budget until we found work, so we wandered round the headland and found the ideal spot – under some upturned rowing boats and out of sight of the police, who, we were told, didn't take kindly to hippies sleeping in the open.

It was Chris who found a job first, at the Rosamar nightclub, just round the corner from where we slept. Chris told me that the Rosamar had another vacancy and, if I was quick, I might get lucky, Sure it wasn't PP's Playground, the raucous discotheque with the girls dancing on the bar and advertised in an iconic photograph in the town square where the waiters were lined up like gunfighters in a spaghetti western. PP's was the place I had my heart set on, but money was in short supply and a job was a job.

I got there in minutes flat and had a brief chat with the head waiter who was in charge of recruitment. He was a tall, angular chain smoker called Pepe. Pepe took an instant dislike to me. For a start there was my hair, it was too long, then the beard and moustache. He didn't say anything about these, he just sniffed and waved his hand in a "No way Jose" kind of manner. Then there were my shoes, brown boots. In the Rosamar, black shoes were mandatory. Pepe made it clear that he didn't like me and told me to go away.

It was Chris's optimism that got me the job.

"Listen, he didn't actually say no. If you get your hair cut, have a shave and put black polish on your boots maybe he'll take you on."

I was desperate for work, so half an hour later found me back at the Rosamar, short haired, clean shaven and wearing freshly blackened boots. I'm still not sure whether Pepe recognised me, but he offered me the job, 1000 pesetas a week, about six pounds, for seven days' work.

The Rosamar was a curious place. It branded itself as a night club, but it was like no other nightclub I have ever seen. It housed about 1500 people who paid around a pound each for the privilege and offered a floor show starring two dancers who were quite the ugliest couple I have ever set eyes on, "El Sali" and his partner Pepita Ibarz. According to the posters, the guitarist was a guy called Paco Pena. I now know that this trio were the crème de la crème of flamenco in the 60s and 70s and played at places like Covent Garden and the Sydney Opera House, but they were not the main attraction. No, the great selling point was that the entrance fee included not only the price of the floor show, but as much champagne as you could drink. Now when I say "champagne" you might think of a nice Veuve Cliquot or a Bollinger, but this stuff was in a league all of its own. The wholesale price was about three pesetas a bottle and was in fact, sour white wine into which some factory in Barcelona had pumped a shed load of gas. It was so awful even I couldn't drink it.

Nevertheless, each night the place was heaving. The doors opened at about seven thirty and every seat was taken up within twenty minutes, tickets having been sold out in advance. My job was to ply the clients with bottles and to make sure everyone was kept fully lubricated. Each night the pattern was the same. After a while, quite a few folks decided they had had enough of a good deal and started ordering more palatable drinks - treble sized shots of spirit for twenty-five pesetas a pop, or a pint of beer for the same price. I never knew what went into the spirits but I sure as hell knew that the triple Bacardis had never been any nearer the Bacardi distillery than I had. The spirits arrived each Thursday by truck from Barcelona in huge glass flagons, each encased in raffia baskets and stoppered with an enormous cork bung. I know this because part of my job was to decant this stuff into the spirit bottles, green stoppers for gin, blue for Bacardi and so on.

After about an hour, things were really rocking, and the pace picked up when the Master of Ceremonies clambered on to the stage and announced that in half an hour the drink service would be suspended when the main act of the evening would commence. The reaction of the crowd was always the same, a moan of collective despair and then everyone waving at me, desperate to get a plentiful supply of anything alcoholic to tide them through the floor show. At this stage in the evening, I felt like a fireman in the blitz trying to put out an unquenchable blaze.

This was what I retrospect you might call the "golden hour", you know the expression, that limited window of opportunity to get someone into the Emergency Room after an accident? Well, my golden hour, or half hour as it so happens, occurred during this frenzy of drinking. By this time, all but the most desperate had forsaken the champagne and were now downing the spirits. I'd take the orders, collect them from the bar, receive payment and, according to the theory pay for the drinks at the till. My wages were so poor that I saw an opportunity to redress the balance by means of keeping most of the cash for myself, but I was always careful to have receipts in my pocket just in case anyone checked up. The first time this happened, Pepe collared me and pulled me to one side.

"I just saw you deliver eight Bacardi and cokes, four gin and tonics and three pints of bitter to table ninety-two, but you never paid for them."

"Yes I did." From my shirt pocket I pulled a receipt for 300 pesetas for the spirits and from my trouser pocket another receipt for 100 pesetas. The sums did not quite match but it was close enough.

"They paid for the spirits and beer separately and they ordered four beers not three. Ask them if you like."

Pepe seemed satisfied.

Eventually the flamenco show began. By this time what little interest anyone had had in it had completely evaporated. Nevertheless, El Sali started, tapping a machine gun beat with his boots. Pepita, meanwhile, swirled and flaunted herself and together there was a certain beauty in their ugliness. As the beat increased, the erotic charge between them grew and, after a series of crescendos, the dance reached a shuddering climax. As it ended there was a moment's stunned silence and then a roar of approval followed immediately by demands for more drink.

The evening ended with the compare announcing, "Good night ladies and gentlemen, guten abend mein damen und herren" and then the music would kick in. Vic Damone crooning 'The Shadow of Your Smile'.

On the way out a group of blokes from Liverpool, it always seemed to be Liverpool, would often walk right through one of the plate glass doors on the upper tier. This wasn't altogether unforeseeable, on account of how much folks had been drinking and the fact that the doors were absolutely transparent. Usually, the wounds were serious enough for the victim to be rushed to hospital but despite me suggesting that warning strips be placed on the glass, nothing was done about it.

On Saturday afternoons wrestling was on the bill. In the morning we would erect the ring, sweating and swearing and racing against time to get things ready. Crowds were slightly smaller than for the evening flamenco, but the deal was similar, free champagne and cheap drink.

I remember the first time I watched a show being surprised by the skills of the wrestlers. One was supposedly a former German paratrooper who entered the ring wearing a World War Two helmet. For two rounds he beat the hell out of "Deaf Mike" from Doncaster. Deaf Mike, an orphan who, as a baby, had been pulled barely alive from his blitzed home, had a number of disadvantages which his Aryan opponent ruthlessly exposed, including falsely signalling by hand gestures that the bell had rung for the end of the round before hitting Deaf Mike with a rabbit punch to the back of the head as he walked to his corner and then hurling him out of the ring. The crowd, understandably, were in uproar.

Happily, Deaf Mike triumphed in the end and the crowd went away happy. After the show, I sat in the bar with the wrestlers and was pleased to see that the rabbit punch had fully restored Deaf Mike's hearing and powers of speech and that the German paratrooper had acquired a Yorkshire accent.

I was settling into life in Spain but, looking back, I'm astonished that I survived those early days. Still, things were improving though that state of affairs was not destined to last long.

Chapter 3
Chickens

I'm running down the street. They're closing in on me, but I know I just have to round the corner, climb the stairs and dive into my bedroom and I'll be home free.

When I wake up, I find myself in prison. Not your ordinary prison, but the sort that nightmares are made of.

I'm lying on my side on the floor and the ceiling is about an inch from my head, so as you can see, I am in a pretty confined space, in fact so confined that I hardly have room to turn. I can see one wall directly in front of me and, if I cast my eyes down, another just beyond where my feet lie.

I'm hot and rather sticky. My mouth tastes like I've eaten something very unpleasant, and my eyes feel as though someone has been using them for pincushions.

I'm numb down my left hand side and so I readjust my position. As I do this, I notice something strange about the ceiling. It seems to be comprised of steel bars, just above which are bits of metal which look rather like springs. I begin to notice other things, including three rugby ball shaped objects lying on the floor which are covered in fluff. These objects seem vaguely familiar but, at this precise moment, I can't quite place them.

With a superhuman effort I manage to twist round and look in the other direction. On the floor beside me is what looks like a suitcase, in fact, it looks like my suitcase. Next to it is a shoe. Gradually my brain begins piecing these images together. It begins to dawn on me that I'm not in prison but seem to be under a bed, my bed in fact. How I got here is a mystery as are the fluff covered rugby balls next to me.

Somehow, I can't remember quite how, I manage to extricate myself from my prison and stand up. My tee-shirt has a rather nasty oil stain on the front which surprises me because I don't remember doing any car repairs in the recent past.

The room contains another bed, in it is Andrew, the Glaswegian. Andrew has two quite serious allergies, work and food. Work has a really bad effect on him and so he lies in bed all day. So far as food is concerned, he has decided to cut down on eating in order to save money. Every day he doesn't eat he reckons that he saves about seventy-five pesetas, about fifty pence. His master plan is to do this for two more months, by which time he figures he will have just enough money to get home. His fallback position is to go and sell blood at Mataro, just outside Barcelona. There you can get 1000 pesetas for an armful. Unfortunately for Andrew, the last time he managed to get there to donate some, he was told that he was so ill he needed a transfusion. So here he is.

Now, you might ask why he wasn't starving and that comes down to something called BUSTAIDS. All of us working in Spain take these drugs. They are designed for slimming and contain enormous quantities of ephedrine which not only depresses your appetite but also gives you the energy to run around for hours on end like the proverbial blue arsed fly. And, being a blue arsed fly is an absolute requirement – hours are long, and wages are low, but this is supposed to be a grand adventure, isn't it?

With Andrew however, the adventure has gone badly wrong because all he now seems to be able to do is to lie in bed and waste away and I think he is already down to about nine stone which isn't good for someone who is over six feet tall. I feel sorry for Andrew and that gets us on to the chickens.

I'd fallen into the habit of going out on the town each night after finishing work in a local bar. As I didn't clock off until about 2 a.m. and this was Spain in the sixties, you can imagine there wasn't much choice. One of the few places to get a drink and continue the party was a place at the back of town called "El Relicario". The place had a huge outdoor garden in which were barrels on trestles and benches packed with foreign workers drinking down flagons of Tinto and Muscatel and covered in red juice from eating Pan Catalan – bread drenched with fresh tomato. I swear that by the end of the evening some of them were literally foaming at the mouth. Meanwhile, in the corner a guy would be toiling in front of an enormous rotisserie which seemed to be hotter than the surface of the sun. Impaled on this must have been twenty or so chickens. In the glare of the fire this was like a scene from an Hieronymus Bosch painting and I am sure Dante must have paid a visit here before he wrote about the inferno.

Curiously, in the garden were some children's swings. I have no idea why they were there because I never saw any kids go anywhere near them. However, they would act on me like a magnet whose force of attraction I couldn't refuse. The first time it happened I remember being turbo charged with some sort of wood alcohol and swinging higher than I had ever swung before and as I did so, I saw the cook remove a sweating chicken from the rotisserie and this gave me an idea, Andrew might like one of those. I launched myself through the air, soared across the garden, landed by the rotisserie, ran half a dozen steps, grabbed the red hot chicken, shoved it into my shirt and legged it down the road.

This became a regular occurrence. Every time it was the same. As I exit a hue and cry begins. My running style is only slightly hampered by the chicken under my shirt which is dripping everywhere. I run quickly downhill and head for home. On this night, however, I'm worried. Behind me are shouts from the Guardia Civil. Those folks don't normally bother with petty crime. Someone must be really upset. The Guardia are dangerous people and I know I mustn't get caught.

Back in the room Andrew fills in some gaps.

"You burst in as usual at about four in the morning, covered in tomato juice and dripping fat everywhere. You briefly said something about the police and dived into bed, but you missed. Your head hit the far wall and you slipped down the side and onto the floor, out of sight. About ten seconds later the door burst open and in steamed three Guardia Civil. They were not happy, they kept mentioning the word 'pollo' and 'ingles', I was a bit confused and wondered what they could possibly want with an English chicken. I finally realised that they were looking for you when they used the word 'idiota.'"

Andrew told them in a combination of bastard Spanish and Glaswegian that yes, an English guy had entered the room – but had dived straight out of the bedroom window which opened on to a flat roof. The police didn't bother to search and bailed out after me. I had had a narrow escape.

"Do you fancy some chicken?" I ask eventually.

Andrew looks pleased.

I fish around under the bed and grab out a rubbery, fluff covered object.

Andrew smiles wanly.

"I think I'll give it a miss if you don't mind" and rummages in his drawer for another Bustaid tablet.

It's more than fifty years since this episode so I've been on the web and, sure enough, El Relicario is still doing a roaring trade in roast chickens. Trip Adviser has some nice things to say, my favourite being:

"i went 2 lloret de mar d uva yr, d nightlife was amazin n im goin bk agen dis august. id recommend goin El Relicario its really gud wiv plenty goin on includin a foam party every Monday"

So, I'm organising my flight and if any of you want to come along just let me know, I'll be at a nearby bar taking bookings.

Chapter 4
Karlobag 78

The coastal road from Rijeka to Split was notorious in those days. Grabbing a lift was difficult at best of times but, as I'd always had luck, we decided to chance it.

Three of us set out that morning, early so as to miss the midday heat. By seven in the morning it was already warming up as we trudged past the docks and out towards the main road south.

I guess we were idiots abroad, Jacko, Tony and me. The other two had never done any hitchhiking so when, after a few minutes, a lift materialised, I generously let them take it. Before they climbed aboard, we hastily agreed a meeting place in Split for later that afternoon.

I found a good place to stand, put my rucksack down and waited. A dribble of cars passed, none of them very fast and none of them very large. I started playing mind games, persuading myself that "I'm sure to get a lift within the next half hour" and when that time came and passed, I changed the rules. "One of the next twenty cars will stop." The only problem was that twenty cars didn't come. By eight thirty almost nothing was moving, and the tarmac was beginning to melt.

I heard it before I saw it. A car, changing gear and accelerating, and then emerging round the bend about five hundred yards away. I stuck out my thumb, stood in the road and flagged it down desperately. The brakes rumbled as the car slowed down.

I opened the passenger door. At the wheel was a young man, bearded and wearing a tee-shirt.

"Split?", I asked.

"Ne, Ne. Samo nekoliko kilometra, deset kilometra."

I looked at my map, I couldn't find anywhere called Samo Nekoliko, or Deset Kilometra. The only place of any significance was Karlobag, some way down the track but I got in anyway, after all, there was no choice. At least I was on my way.

We drove up out of Rijeka and all was well with the world. We had the windows open and bathed in the warm draft that flowed through the car.

My guide kept trying to ask me something,

"Voda?, voda?" and mimed taking a drink.

I thought it was rather early and anyway far too hot for a drink of vodka and so I said no. He looked concerned and asked me again:

"Ne, imate li vode? ....Voda, voda?"

Voda? Of course, that's what he's asking, "Yes" I replied vigorously, "I have a father", I smiled and gave him a thumbs up.

My new-found friend seemed delighted at this news and smiled back broadly.

He pointed to a track up ahead and said something else which I couldn't understand. The car slowed and the penny dropped. This was where he was turning off. Not as good a lift as I'd hoped for, maybe twenty kilometres or so but better than nothing.

I waved goodbye to him and saw the car trundling down the track towards the sea, bluer than blue and sparkling in the distance. From here on I was on my own.

Now that I was no longer moving, I became aware of just how hot it was. I parked my rucksack by the side of the road and waited for another car to come, but after a few minutes decided that I might as well start walking; at least the breeze of my own movement might help keep me cool.

The road climbed steadily and, after about half an hour, I saw, down to my right, a collection of three or four small houses. This was the first sign of life I'd seen since the car disappeared. As I got closer, I noticed a group of young men near the road. I waved as I approached. They didn't wave back. One of them yelled something quite aggressively.

"Odjebi"

I later discovered that this word has something to do with both travel and reproduction but, in ignorance, I waved and smiled.

One of them, the leader perhaps, picked up a large stone and threw it at me. The others followed suit. I have to say I was quite annoyed about this especially when one flew past my year and hit my rucksack.

Sod this for a game of soldiers, I thought, and I picked up a smooth stone, about the size of a walnut. I threw it at the biggest of the group and it struck a rock by the side of his head. This was not a clever thing to do because an immediate fusillade of missiles rained down on me.

I decided it was best to get a move on.

I picked up my pace, crossed over the brow of the hill and soon left the incident behind.

I was now beginning to feel thirsty.

Mmm, I could do with some water. What was the Yugoslavian for water, I wondered? Still, not to worry, I'll get some when I get to Split.

I carried on walking. Up ahead I could see the road rising once more. It seemed to reach a high point about two miles away. I was sure that a car would come by and pick me up before I got there but, nevertheless, I carried on walking.

It was now baking hot and perfectly quiet apart from the intermittent sound of cicadas. They were silent for long periods and then suddenly they would go absolutely ape shit. After a while this began to get to me. My mouth was dry, so I stopped to look in my rucksack to see if I had anything to quench my thirst but only located a half finished packet of salted peanuts.

I looked at my watch. I saw two things. Firstly, it was eleven o'clock, and secondly, there was a white mark where my watch strap had been. I was already beginning to burn.

I was beginning to feel rather isolated, exposed and worried. There was no traffic at all on the road and I realised that any sensible person would put off travelling until it became cooler in late afternoon. In the meantime, I was stuck on a mountain with no shade, no water, and no prospects of any rescue until the evening.

As this thought was sinking in, I rounded the bend and saw a small collection of white houses, towards the coast on my right. From these, a track rose towards the main road, and, on the track, something was moving. I could see the sunlight bouncing off metal and then I heard the unmistakable sound of a tractor's diesel engine as it climbed towards the junction with the main road about one and a half miles ahead of me. In a fraction of a second I'd sized the situation up. If I could get to the junction before the tractor I would jump on board. I didn't care how far the tractor was going but at least it would get me out of this hole.

I started to run, downhill at first and then through a cutting where, for a short time, I lost sight of the tractor. When I emerged the tractor was much higher and closer to the road than I had hoped. I could hear its engine distinctly straining as it began the last and steepest part of the climb. I was also climbing, running like a man possessed, I was going to make it.

The tractor changed gear, and I saw blue smoke issue from its exhaust. I was close now, perhaps three hundred yards from the junction, but the tractor was even closer. And I could clearly make out the driver sitting there smoking, completely oblivious to me.

I got to within seventy-five yards of the junction as the tractor turned onto the main road and continued up the hill ahead of me. It was in its lowest gear, and I was gaining and yelling frantically, but the noise of the tractor drowned everything out. As it crested the hill I was so close I felt I could touch it, but once over the top, gravity took over and it gradually drew away from me, slowly at first then more and more rapidly. I could have cried.

I walked on but had no real plan of action. I looked at my watch and it was past noon, the hottest part of the day. Down to my right, just off the road, were some thorn bushes. These gave me an idea. I scrambled down to them, and took my towel out of my rucksack, removed my tee-shirt and scooped a hole beneath them. With my clothes I made a canopy which provided a little shade. I got a spare shirt and covered my head and lay in the depression that I had scraped out and found a little shelter from the blistering sun.

I lay there until almost two o'clock. It was uncomfortable, boring and hot but, on reflection, it was a pretty good idea.

When I could stand it no longer, I got dressed, packed my bag and got back on the road.

A few minutes later, the road passed through another cutting, the marble sides of which behaved like a parabolic mirror focusing the whole force of the sun on me. As I breathed in my lungs felt as though they were on fire.

It was then I saw it, a rusting road sign frying in the blistering heat. All it said was "Karlobag 78".

Seventy - eight kilometres. "Holy shit, that's fucking miles. I'm completely fucked."

I dragged myself forward.

As I exited the cutting, I noticed a narrow footpath leading higher up the hill to the left of the road. To me this meant one thing, a house, and a house meant water.

The path entered the shade of a stand of pine trees, and as it did so, the temperature fell slightly. As the path rose, so did my spirits. Within a few minutes I saw a building with a small courtyard surrounded by a low stone wall. In the centre of the courtyard was a well and I could almost hear and smell the water. As I reached courtyard gate I was aware of a buzzing sound and saw that the court contained half a dozen beehives and that the air was full of flying insects. I yelled out to see if there was anybody at home but got no reply. I had a dilemma. Should I brave the bees and try get to the water or should I return to the road?

Reluctantly, and after a couple of minutes' hesitation, I made my way back downhill.

I wasn't sure how long I could go on like this. My lips were cracking, my face was scorched, and the day just seemed to be getting hotter and hotter.

I went forward through another cutting and again I saw a path, so similar to the last one that, at first, I thought the heat was making me hallucinate. This time I'd made my mind up, if I found water I was having it no matter what. Again, I saw a small house, again there was a courtyard with beehives and again there was a well.

This time there was a difference. In the courtyard, sitting on a deckchair was a man wearing a pair of wire glasses and swimming trunks. He was a picture of relaxation, quietly reading a book. I called out to him.

"Please, can I have some water?"

"Voda? Yes, yes voda, kommen sie in, kommen sie in."

I walked to the well. There was a rope attached to a metal bucket.

I dropped it some twenty feet to the water below. It made a delicious splash. The bucket tipped to one side and filled to the brim. The water in it shone like quicksilver. I pulled the rope and hauled up the bucket.

I raised it and emptied the entire contents over my head. The relief was incredible. My host burst into laughter and said "Wait!". He disappeared into the house and emerged clutching a camera.

"Again", he said, "do it again, bitte." I emptied another bucket over my head as he took photographs laughing all the time.

The third bucket I drank. I guess it must have held about half a gallon, but it only took about ten minutes to consume all of it.

The man had disappeared again, and this time re-emerged with a plate of bread, cheese and tomatoes.

"Essen. Is gut ja?"

"Thank you, thank you," I said. "Danke schoen."

"Not Deutsch, Jugoslavien," he said and took another couple of pictures.

"Where do you go?"

"Split."

"There is garage in two, three kilometres, maybe you get lift there."

I nodded my thanks and felt that it was time to go.

My host hugged me and gave me a bag of black grapes and stood by the gate waving as I walked away, back down the footpath.

About half an hour later I reached the garage at a small road junction. It was, in reality, a shed with a petrol pump. Outside was a small Fiat 500 parked in the shade, while inside, the owner, a young woman, was enjoying a drink at the only table in the place.

I was always nervous about asking people for a lift but, on that day, I walked up to her and asked straight out if she was going my way.

"Yes", she replied, "But only as far as Karlobag." I could have kissed her.

In my many years of hitchhiking that was perhaps the best lift I've ever had.

I made it to Split around ten thirty that night having caught a bus the remainder of the way, and the rest of that summer is, as they say, history.

A few years ago, I returned to the Croatian coast in the height of summer and, in the course of a few weeks, drove up and down that stretch of road several times. The main thing that struck me was just how much traffic there is these days. The Karlobag signpost is long gone, as is the garage. Interestingly, I didn't see a single hitchhiker. Perhaps though, I If had looked under a thorn bush, I might have seen one or two sheltering from the heat.

Chapter 5
Joni Mitchell, the Prime Minister and the Exploding Freak

It all started a day or two after the Karlobag incident, following which I'd survived a robbery attempt, Jacko had acquired some interesting, knitted woollen swimming trunks which behaved alarmingly when wet, and we had spent the night in a public toilet escaping a torrential downpour.

Tony saw them first, across the beach at Dubrovnik, a tall blonde woman and her companion, young and slim with short dark hair.

We waved, they waved back, and a while later we bumped into them in a bar on the sea front.

It transpired that they too were heading for Greece, taking the five p.m. sailing from Dubrovnik to Igoumenitsa. The blonde woman was Veronique and her friend, Andree. They were French Canadiennes, both a few years older than us and both getting away from things back home.

It was clear from the get-go that Tony had designs on Veronique and that his intentions were reciprocated.

I don't remember when the idea of going to Matala came up, but I'm pretty sure it was within a few minutes of boarding the ship.

Jacko had already commented that the two women were reading some "weird shit" and sure enough, they seemed to have about twenty kilos' worth of the works of Krishnamurti and I think that this had a lot to do with their plans.

I remember Andree talking about eastern mysticism and informing me that she was on a voyage of discovery before showing me a photocopy of an article in Life magazine – all about hippies living in a cave in southern Crete and "getting back to nature". I was immediately grabbed by the idea – but, if truth be told, I was really more interested in the tales of the drugs and laid back lifestyle than anything more spiritual. Andree obviously saw a spark of interest and she smiled, looked into my eyes, put her hand on my thigh and said those immortal words, "You have eyes like a Canadian forest," before thrusting a copy of 'Freedom from the known' into my hands.

We didn't head straight to Crete but spent a few days hitching to Athens before catching a ferry to Chania and sleeping on the beach at Platania. From there we split up for a few days, Tony, Jacko and I heading south down the Samaria Gorge from Omalos to Aghia Roumelli before taking a boat to Chora Sfakion, eventually travelling by bus back north to Rethymnon, and then back south to Aghia Gallini.

I remember the last couple of miles into Matala. The bus was about two thirds full – mainly young folks – all headed to find a cave in which to while away the summer. As we got nearer the coast the road narrowed, while on our right hand side the rushes grew to an amazing height alongside a dried up river bed. On our left the rock walls held a sprinkling of caves – some with wooden shutters and doors, a few with glass windows and clearly these were still inhabited by locals.

The bus pulled to a halt on a patch of dirt at the edge of a beach. About twenty or so people had wandered up to take a look at the newest arrivals and perhaps to reconnect with acquaintances that they had met elsewhere on the road. Others accompanied people who were leaving. Tears were shed. Hugs were exchanged and kisses donated.

The men were all clad in shorts – almost no one had a shirt, and the women wore a variety of clothes – some wore shorts, others bikinis and others tie die robes. A lot of folks wore those multi coloured beads that came from Morocco, possession of which was proof of membership of the hippie community.

As I got off the bus I felt rather like Neil Armstrong stepping off the LEM into the unknown. Everyone watching seemed self-assured, but we were newcomers. Almost immediately however, a Glaswegian guy, Tommy, opened up a conversation - asking where we were from and then introducing us to some of his friends. He showed us the beach tap from which we could shower and said he would see us later at the Dolphin- one of just a couple of bars that then existed in Matala.

We strolled west along the beach towards a biscuit coloured headland that was covered in caves, lay our rucksacks on the ground and dived into the milk warm waters of the Libyan Sea.

Days ran into each other, and the days ran into weeks and life was good. I managed to earn a bit of money by collecting beer bottles from the beach – money which was spent getting out of it at the Dolphin Restaurant. I heard later that someone called Joni Mitchell had once held court at the only other bar in town, the Mermaid, but, although it was only about 100 yards away, I never quite made it that far.

I might have missed Joni, but I did witness the spectacle of the incredible exploding freak. The freak was a strange guy. No one ever heard him speak and he seemed to exist solely on a diet of drugs and alcohol. Rumour had it that his real name was George, he was from a very well connected family and that he had been born and educated in the USA.

That day started off like any other with us hauling ourselves to the Dolphin for a late morning sharpener. There were about twenty or so of us in there when the owner, Harris, tried to shoo us to the back of the restaurant. He was expecting a tour bus which was an unheard of occurrence. We were not best pleased to be shifted and the freak looked distinctly edgy. He didn't like surprises especially after the episode in which he had accidentally downed half a coke bottle of homemade acid a few days before and had, as a result, developed an odd twitch and a million mile stare.

Once we had been moved, Harris laid a long trestle table and set about thirty places. At intervals were bowls of Greek salad, loaves of bread and bottles of retsina.

Just after midday the tourists arrived. Their tour guide spoke to them in English. He invited them to take as many photos of the hippies (us) as they liked before sitting down to eat.

The freak clearly didn't like being objectified and his twitch began to kick in, big time.

Almost as soon as they sat down the freak struggled to his feet and, with an agility that astounded me, he leapt on to the table. He then ran from one end to the other, arms swinging like a chimpanzee. As he ran, he swept up items of food and shoved them into his mouth and, seizing a bottle of retsina, he downed a half litre in one long draught.

By the time he had got to the far end he had somehow lost his trousers, and as he turned to complete a return trip, not only was Greek salad on display but also a sizeable portion of meat and two veg accompanied by a pair of sunburnt buttocks sporting a tattoo of a lion.

On the return leg, the freak picked up speed – and more food and drink. You might have thought that the tour group would have scattered but they didn't. They sat there transfixed – as if they were witnessing some pagan hippie rite – which, in a way, I guess they were.

On his third lap, the freak gathered even more pace. By this time, what with the olive oil and stuff spilt all over the table, his footing was giving everyone cause for concern.

Suddenly, he skidded to a halt, stood up straight, raised his arms to the heavens and swallow dived off the table and over the low wall which separated the restaurant from the beach. As he took flight fountains erupted from both ends. It was a performance that I think, in later years, the likes of Cirque de Soleil would have been proud of.

I've been back to Matala a few times in the past ten years and so it was that in 2019 I found myself back in the Dolphin Restaurant where I saw a face I thought I recognised, a silver haired guy, about my age, with a mad look in his eye. He was sitting in the freak's favourite seat. The waitress caught my eye and asked quietly if I knew the man on the next table. I said I thought so but wasn't certain. She lowered her voice and let me in on the fact that lots of people seemed to recognise him and it might be George Papandreou the former Greek Prime Minister. I laughed, I thought she was joking but on taking another look I realised she was serious.

I got up and walked over. I was about to ask the question that dare not speak its name but before I could the man gave a twitch, shook my hand, smiled, and in a North American drawl said,

"I'm George, haven't we met before somewhere?"

Chapter 6
Don

Don was the sort of guy you would see all the time in those days. He had long, lank hair and a beard that looked as though it was stuck on and made of the sort of stuff that you use to fill sofas.

Hilary and I met him just outside of Heilbronn. He was leaning against a road sign on the autobahn slip road, kitbag by his side. He was hitchhiking in an aimless sort of way, I guess.

"Hi," he said, and, after a short pause while he drew on a rather large home- made cigarette,

"It is good we speak English, no?"

We nodded and agreed.

"You live in England, ja?"

"Yes, what about you?"

He smiled. "Ich lebe in Deutschland." Then, after a long pause,"It is best I go to Dusseldorf. There are many Schwefelsäure-Fabriken in Dusseldorf."

Another pause. He must have seen that I was puzzled.

"Schwefelsäure-Fabriken...in English you are saying....Sulphuric Acid Factories, yes?"

I nodded. I was still a bit bewildered but figured that something must have got lost in translation.

Hilary and I wandered along the road, dropped our rucksacks and stuck out our thumbs. Hitching as a couple was always easy in those days and, an hour later, we were being dropped outside the students' union at Heidelberg University. I'd stayed there several times before on my way to and from Greece or Yugoslavia, and, on each occasion, had a fine time. True to form, the university found us a place to crash out for a couple of nights on the top floor of a grey, concrete student accommodation block.

It was already partially occupied by a couple of Irish guys called, believe it or not, Pat and Mick. They were delighted when I told them that I knew the ropes around there and had been invited to the opening-night of the student bar for the start of the new academic year and even more pleased when I let them in on the fact that we had been promised free beer.

We were about to head out when Don reappeared.

"Is good I again meet you," he said in his strange accent.

"Where are you from?" Pat asked.

"Ich lebe in Deutschland but ich bin ein American."

Holy hell! this guy was an American. I would never have guessed. I figured he must either be a recent immigrant or had suffered some traumatic brain injury, otherwise his English would not have been so tortured.

As I looked across to him he began rolling yet another large cigarette.

We spent the next three days with these guys. Contrary to our initial impression, Don's first language was English but, fuelled by drugs and ignorance, he had developed a novel approach to learning German. He explained it like this:

"It is best that I am forgetting all my English to learn like a baby. So, I'm not speak English for funf months. I live in Svansea, in caravan. Ist gut, in Svansea, no one speak Englisch."

From this I deduced that Don had been on some sort of English language destruction course and, fuelled by vast quantities of drugs, it seemed to have worked pretty well for him. He now seemed to have reduced his native English to almost zero and was endeavouring to replace everything with new German grammar and vocabulary.

"Every day it is good I have ten German words, new."

He flourished a very tattered paperback English-German dictionary and a blue notebook. He opened the latter.

"Yesterday it was sulphuric acid, today it is, petrol, ...benzin, tin plate, zinnplatt, combine harvester, grape, headroom, pound, slowcoach und syphilis. Ist gut ya?

"How do you choose which words to learn?" I asked.

"Is best to do random" and showed us. He opened the dictionary, closed his eyes and stabbed at the page with his biro, it landed on "cigarette lighter" – "zigarettenanzünder".

I studied Don's revolutionary "learn a language through ignorance" technique quite closely.

One night in the bar he was engaging in conversation with a crowd of German students. I noticed that the less English Don spoke, the more I understood. The same, however, was not necessarily true of his audience.

His opening gambit was always the same. Discovering that one member of his audience was from Hamburg, Don asked,

"Haben Sie ein gross Schwefelsäure Fabriken in Hamburg?"

After some initial puzzlement, came the reply:

"No, we don't have a big sulphuric acid factory in Hamburg."

Undaunted, Don pressed on.

"Haben sie Syphilis?"

A young woman choked on her beer.

Almost without a pause Don continued, "In Port Talbot gibt es ein zinnplatte fabrik, Ja?"

It was interesting to note that although all Don's questions were in German the answers were invariably in English. Don was aware of this but seemed undaunted.

It was shortly after an abortive conversation about combine

harvesters that the Americans arrived from the nearby army base. Loud, aggressive, drunk and full of national pride they immediately got up my nose. Don, whom we had discovered was originally from Detroit, seemed particularly ill at ease. Perhaps it had something to do, I reflected later, with his gnomic statement "it is best I go to Canada in 1970".

In 1970 the Vietnam War was at its height and many young Americans opposed it and fled to Canada to avoid the draft. The American soldiers though seem to have had no misgivings. After all, they were safe in Europe and were full of macho pride about what they were doing to the "VC over there".

Don became more withdrawn as the evening wore on. Eventually, he excused himself. Waving his cigarette lighter he said loudly

"Ich need Benzin für meinen zigarettenanzünder."

On his way out he put a coin into the juke box and left as the opening bars of a Bob Dylan song kicked in.

My memory of what happened next is quite hazy, but I do recall the arrival of the fire engines and then the soldiers going apeshit.

In the car park, four military vehicles were quietly smouldering. Looking around I realised that the only person missing on the scene was Don.

No one was sure what happened, but they say it happened very quick and that almost no one saw anything, in fact the only person who might have known something was a bearded hitchhiker seen at a nearby roundabout with a handwritten sign which said "Dusseldorf Bitte".

Chapter 7
The Fall

The map indicated two options, "*Route Normale*" and "*Passage Dangereux*". When I read this, I laughed and thought of double entendres. As a lifelong sufferer of vertigo, I knew that the "*Route Normale*" was enough for me.

I was on the penultimate day of a solo walking tour in the Alps. I was strong and fit and was enjoying meeting other folks on the route. Some days earlier I had encountered Tom and Andrew, two British kids aged about sixteen, who were following roughly the same route as me, and we had set out together from the refuge after breakfast.

That morning was a thing of beauty. Crystalline air, bright alpine flowers and paths weaving in and out of the forest before reaching the high plateau which offered spectacular views of the Mer De Glace and town of Chamonix on the glaciated valley floor way, way below.

We talked as we walked, making excellent progress, and the miles ticked away. Gradually, however, the path began to narrow and soon it was reduced to the width of a pavement, hemmed in between a sheer rock wall on our right and a rather worrying two thousand foot drop on the left. For most people this would not have presented a problem, I mean it's not often that folks fall off something as wide as a pavement is it? However, as I mentioned, I'm not really normal as far as heights go and the feeling of exposure made me feel distinctly unwell. My discomfort increased dramatically when we rounded a bend to find the path coming to a dead end.

Above the path, rising very steeply, was a rock wall, hammered to which, about eight inches from the surface, was an iron banister.

The idea was to climb up, using the banister to haul on. The rock was smooth – worn by innumerable mountain boots, while at the base was a sheer drop. I felt even more unwell.

I decided to consult the map. In seconds I realised our error. Right at the beginning of the day we had somehow missed the track to the *Route Normale* and now we were at the foot of the *Passage Dangereux*.

Now, there's something about a name, it sort of gives you a clue about the person, the place or the object. So, I'm figuring "*Normale*" means OK, right? but a path which is described as "*Dangereux*" means it's probably the go to place for folks with a death wish.

So here I am, and I have some choices, go back for two hours and try to find the safer route or scare myself shitless. Tom and Andrew can see my discomfort and are happy to walk back with me if necessary.

"It's your decision" Tom says.

Just as he says this the Von Trapp family appear. They are climbing down the rock from above and moving at quite a pace. There are four of them. A mother, father and two children aged about nine and seven, I guess. They aren't really singing the hit songs from the "Sound of Music" nor are they wearing lederhosen, but they might as well be. They smile as they skip past us on the outside of our narrow ledge and wave gaily as they go on their way.

My mind was made up. "If those kids can do it then so can I," I said and immediately wanted to vomit.

The young lads went first, making their way steadily upward. I waited until they were clear of the bottom, then tightened my rucksack, gripped the banister and started to climb.

You know, it's really odd when you are high up, how acutely you notice the sounds of the wind. I don't know whether it's because your senses are on high alert but, on that day, it seemed terrifying. Not loud, not powerful, but sinister, cold and erratic; calm one moment, crying and tugging menacingly at me the next.

I had progressed about fifteen feet when the first crisis occurred. My right foot slipped just as I was moving one hand up the banister, I was thrown off balance and my rucksack swung round and clouted the rock. Luckily my other hand still had a firm grip and, although a terrible thrill ran through my body, I held on. I then did a silly thing. I couldn't help myself. I looked down. Below my feet the slope dropped away into nothingness, and I convulsed with fear as my vertigo kicked in. The rock wall spun crazily, and I felt the whole mountain turning upside down. My hands were sweating, and my terror was so great I almost willed myself to let go and end it all. I think all of this must have lasted no more than a few seconds but for me it was a lifetime. My arms felt weak, and I didn't know if I'd be able to move, but eventually, through sheer force of will, I got going and, after a few minutes, hauled myself to the top.

The boys were waiting for me on a narrow path and patted me on the back. I swore and laughed and swore some more.

"Thank fuck that's over; I am never, ever doing anything like that again. Never."

After a few minutes we shouldered our bags and rounded the corner. It was then I realised that I was in deep shit because another sheer wall faced us, only this time it was about three times as long as the previous pitch.

I sat down on the ledge.

"I don't think I can do this."

I looked at the alternatives. There weren't many. Going back down the ladder would be even more terrifying than going up, so that was out. I'm not kidding, I thought seriously about feigning a heart attack and calling in a Mountain Rescue helicopter but, after an agonising pause, I realised that I had to go on.

My companions were concerned for my safety and could clearly see the state I was in. They had hatched out a plan to help me. Andrew said, "Tom will take the lead, you follow, and I'll be right below you. If you fall, I'll catch you."

This was a wonderful gesture, the sort you get in those old World War Two movies where the hero sacrifices himself for his friends. The only problem was the fact that I knew that if I tumbled off the mountain, whoever was below me would be knocked off as well.

So, it was settled. Tom would go first, followed by Andrew while I'd bring up the rear.

I stood up. "Let's go."

The others seemed surprised at my eagerness, but, if truth be told, I couldn't stand the tension any more.

At the bottom of the pitch the boys made doubly sure I was up for the climb and then one by one they set off, ascending slowly and steadily and without a word being spoken.

The first step was hard, but I forced myself to take it. Again, I could hear and feel the wind whistling around my head and could feel the pull of the empty space beneath me. After half a dozen steps my hands felt slippery on the steel banister but I was too frightened to try to wipe them. I was concentrating fiercely, just focusing on the next move. In my fear I was climbing too fast and quickly I was within inches of Andrew's boots on the rock above me and I had to stop. As I did, the wind seemed to pick up and my hands seemed to be drenched in sweat. In my ears I could hear the roar of blood and my heart was racing like crazy.

I managed to speak above the noise of the wind.

"Please can you move a bit quicker?" The unsaid message was "I'm about to fall off so, whatever happens, don't stop."

After this hiatus Andrew speeded up and I now felt the distance between us grow and this made me feel even more uncomfortable. I was beginning to feel out on a limb so to speak when I heard a cry from above. This was followed by a skittering of small stones that bounced down the rock, pelting my face like hail. There was another cry, "Look out!" and a small boulder came lolloping towards me, bouncing and leaping. Instinctively I pressed my face down and the object sailed past my head, striking my rucksack and almost dragging me off the slab. The vertigo kicked in again. I shut my eyes while the universe span and twisted all around. As I began to calm down my right knee took on a life of its own, it was trembling violently and bashing itself against the rock wall. This alarmed me but not so much as the thought that, unless the trembling calmed down, I could not climb. I also knew that there was a limit to how long I'd be able to maintain my grip on the banister.

I became aware of a voice above me, Andrew. He had apparently been calling to see if I was OK, but I hadn't heard him.

I was desperately thinking of how to find a way out of this mess. A trick I used to use when running marathons was to fool my body into doing things it didn't want to. One example is the short run trick. When you've run twenty miles and are completely exhausted and you have another six miles to go you say to yourself "six miles is just like a short training run. You've done it hundreds of times, you can easily do it once more."

While I was thinking this, I noticed my right leg was wet through and this made my mind up. I told myself,

"Just climb ten steps, anyone can do that."

I started. After ten steps I was feeling better.

"Best make it twenty."

Then

"I'm going to do a hundred and then rest."

The interesting thing was I knew that if I rested, I'd get the terrors all over again, but I had to kid part of myself that I was going to stop.

As I climbed higher, I began to feel that I just might reach the top. But then what? – were there other pitches to come?

I looked up. Fifteen feet ahead were two pairs of boots dangling over the edge. The owners, Tom and Andrew were obviously sitting down but I couldn't see the rest of their bodies. I made a final push and levered myself on to the path above. We were at the top.

I fell forward and was overcome by a blinding headache and couldn't stand for about fifteen minutes.

I've done the tour de Mont Blanc a few times since that day and each time have avoided the *Passage Dangereux*. In fact, most walking books now refer to that section simply as "the ladders". Looking at a YouTube video whilst writing this, the climb looked even worse than I remembered and even though nowadays there is much more protection in place, the yawning chasm beneath the climb is still terrifying.

PART TWO: AUSTRALIA

"Do you come from a land down under
Where women glow and men plunder
Can't you hear, can't you hear the thunder?
You better run, you better take cover."

Men at Work

Chapter 8
Shoot Out at Seal Rocks

A small low developed approximately 200 km east-northeast of Townsville on 11 January and then moved north northeast and slowly deepened during the next two days. The low reached its most northern position approximately 250 km north northeast of Willis Island at 0000 UTC 13 January and then moved southwards with cyclone status being reached at 0300 UTC 14 January.

At 1600 UTC 16 January, Frederick Reef (AWS) reported the strongest wind speed of 130 km/h and a pressure of 991.5 hPa when Grace was located 60 km to the west.

Severe Tropical Cyclone Grace, 11 - 20 January 1984. Australian Government Bureau of Meteorology

The air is thick like honey and sticks to my skin.

To my left there's a wide sweep of beach, to the right a low rocky promontory. On the sand, near a boat, there is a ferocious buzz around the slack jawed carcass of a fish and a thumb sized fly is perched on one of its eyes.

The wind riffles something on the beach, some sort of plastic sacking with faded writing, bleached by the rain, wind and sun.

I notice a group of cars heading out of town –it seems as though everyone is leaving but me. Still, I figure, if things get bad – I can always crash out in the pub.

Getting there had not been a problem. It was, after all, a holiday weekend and the traffic was brisk. Leaving Sydney, I got a lift with a guy who trained racehorses for a living. He dropped me by the turn off at Boolambayte, from where I guessed it was about thirty Ks to

Seal Rocks. It was just after midday so there was still a bit of traffic. Within a few minutes a truck carrying beer supplies stopped and I climbed aboard.

We rolled down a dirt road through the rain forest listening to the strains of Today FM punctuated by warnings of a tropical cyclone, all the while getting tantalising glimpses of the wide blue Pacific and its famous surf breaks through gaps in the trees.

After about half an hour we reached the shoreline and pulled up outside the Seal Rocks Hotel. I thanked my friend for the lift, climbed down and set off in search of the campground.

When I arrived, everyone, it seemed, had gone. Bad news about bad weather travels fast I guess.

I found a good spot and dropped my tent.

"Jeez, its goin' to blow like a bastard."

The voice came from an old guy living in an old caravan parked in a sheltered spot under a cliff overhang at the back of the park.

"G'day, how you doin? I'm Bill. Happened like this in '73, blew like bejeesus for three days, and washed everything out. You sleeping in that?" he said, pointing to my tent, a red plastic thing not really waterproof, but light and cheap.

"She'll be in tatters within the hour, best drag your gear into my place."

"Thanks all the same but I reckon I'll be fine."

I finished putting my tent up, stored my rucksack inside, put on my board shorts and headed across a small strip of tarmac towards the beach.

As I did, I noticed more people on their way out.

Back on the beach there's sweat in the air and the water's unnaturally low. Off to the right a flash of lightening followed seconds later by a long rolling boom like gunfire. Out at sea there's an enormous wall of blackness, terrifying. I'd seen storms before, but this was altogether different.

The sea, however, was behaving normally, just a one metre swell and this relaxed me; after all it wasn't as if a typhoon was roaring in, was it?

As soon as I had this thought the wind began to pick up. Not too much, but with it came the first gobs of rain. As I looked again out to sea I saw a dark, dense curtain moving rapidly towards me.

I turned and ran towards my tent. Time to hunker down. I dove in and lay on top of my sleeping bag. Seconds later the rain hit the tent with biblical force. For a moment everything was okay, and then a little leak appeared in the corner, not surprising really. A sudden gust of wind and the tent billowed like a parachute. Another gust, this time even stronger and by now the floor of the tent had begun rippling in the areas where I was not in touch with the ground.

The tent was really small with no room to stand up, so I lay down and, unable to do anything else, tried to read my book, "The Glass Bead Game" by Hermann Hesse. If truth be told, I wasn't really enjoying it very much, As the title says it's about the Glass Bead Game, which is beautiful, intricate and basically pointless, which just about summed up my view of the book.

The wind outside was howling and when I looked through my tent flap I could see stuff flying everywhere, air beds, trash cans, buckets, paper and plastic bags and the occasional article of swimwear.

I lay down again and waited for the wind to subside, but it didn't. My problems started to mount when the tent pegs began lifting out of the ground and the whole thing threatened to take off. More water began coming in, tons of it. I don't know if you've ever seen the film "Das Boot" – the one about the German U-boat that had more leaks than a Welsh allotment - well, by this stage I was feeling pretty much like the U-Boat's Chief Engineer fighting a one man war against the water.

The light suddenly dimmed and then the noise of the wind rose to a high pitched shriek; something hard hit the side of the tent, tearing a jagged hole through which I could see absolute turmoil. Quickly I stuffed my gear into my rucksack and made a dash for a place of greater safety.

Outside in the storm I realised just what a predicament I was in. Where to go? The pub was an option, but it was too far away. What about the old bloke's caravan – was that still standing? Yes, there it was, under the rock overhang.

I ran, fighting against the elements, dragging my sodden gear with me. I banged on the van door. It opened almost immediately.

"Tent's gone then?'

I nodded

"Come in, quick and get that wet gear off."

The van was buffeting and bouncing like a lifeboat out at sea.

"Tucker, mate?"

I realised I hadn't eaten since breakfast, so I nodded as I stripped off and towelled myself down.

Bill smiled, "She's set in for a few days. The main highway's out and Lauriton's flooded."

Bill had elicited this fact from small transistor radio perched on one of the shelves.

Lauriton was three hours north, so this was a big storm.

"She's gusting at over 120 miles an hour" he said with a hint of delight. "She's tearing the coast to pieces. We're goin' to be here for a few days mate, so you might as well make yourself at home."

He handed me a plate of baked beans and a cup of tea.

"There'll be nothing down here for at least a week," he continued, scratching his rear and looking rather pleased with his pronouncement.

"What a bastard," he said and, as shrapnel flew past, he smiled once more.

I was beginning to see a pattern. The more dire the pronouncement, the happier Bill seemed. At that moment he was in seventh heaven.

"You can kip there," he said, pointing to a long cushioned seat by the table.

Inside the van, I noticed a book shelf populated with cowboy pulp fiction sandwiched between a couple of huge catering packs of baked beans.

Bill saw me looking at the books. "Like a good read, do you?"

"Yeah," I replied.

"What do you think of this?"

He passed me a tattered paperback, "Murder at Poison Wells".

I opened it and read the opening passage,

"Burl Wilson spat into the dirt. That rat, Tod Ellinger was going to pay for this. He ran his hand over the smooth metal barrel of his Colt Cavalry revolver. He admired its engraved surface and span the chamber with the palm of his hand. Its heft felt welcome and its weight told him that it was fully loaded and ready for business."

"I've got a whole collection."

There must have been over a hundred. "Rustlers of the Purple Sage", "Shootout at Pistol Ridge", "The Siren of Rattlesnake Creek", "Bury my saddle at Brumby Gulch",

"I've read all of these. Fancy trading?" Bill looked at me hopefully.

"I've only got one." I dug out my Herman Hesse novel and passed it over.

We sat down with our books as the storm howled around.

"The finely tooled boots of Tod Ellinger tattooed on the sidewalk. It was kill, or be killed, and the hard eyed stranger meant to live."

I had just read these immortal words when Bill raised a buttock off the seat and noisily added to the atmospheric disturbance.

He then let rip a salvo of comments, fired like bullets from Todd Ellinger's hand gun:

"Who is this bloody idiot, Hesse? Wasn't he a war criminal or something. Whatever, he should be shot for writing shit like this. When does the girl appear? And if he wants this glass bead thing so bad why doesn't he just shoot someone and take it?"

By ten o'clock I had been to Wombat Wells, survived snake bites and was just entering Brumby Gulch when I noticed something.

Bill was lying on his back, snoring from both ends. The van was otherwise still and quiet. I got up and went outside. What struck me was the silence and then the sky. The clearest I've ever seen; a near perfect circle of stars surrounded by a ring of blackness.

I woke Bill and we went out again. We looked in awe, the eye of the storm. Dead still, dead calm and dead silent. I made a brew and we wandered to the shore. The sea was streaked with the phosphorescent trails of phytoplankton while above us swirled the Southern Cross, the Big Dipper and the diamond trail of the Milky Way. Even now I cannot really describe the scene but Bill, in his own way, summed it up

"I'll be buggered."

We stayed there until we felt a breeze stirring and knew that, once the eye passed over, the full fury of the storm would be visited on us again, and so it was that even before we got back to the van, twigs and leaves were again flying through the air.

We stayed together in the van for four more days, eventually running out of cooking gas and having to use the Glass Bead Game to light camp fires under our rock overhang.

The minor roads were still washed out on the day I left, to walk the thirty clicks to the main highway.

Bill walked me as far as the end of town.

He shook my hand. "Time to saddle up old hoss and head for the Alamo. There's a wide range out there jest waiting fer you."

I turned and headed inland. As I crested the first rise, I saw Bill raise his arm to me in farewell and I made my mind up that one day I'd send Bill an addition to his collection of stories describing our shoot out at Seal Rocks.

Chapter 9
Cauliflower

I woke with a terrible headache and about a kilo of loose change and damp five dollar notes in my trouser pockets.

After breakfast I wandered into town, stunned by the cobalt sky which I imagine could, under certain conditions, make you want to thrash paint all over a canvass or sever your ear. There was no breath of wind, and it was already hot as I entered the main store to buy a few bits and pieces. Although the choice was limited I managed to find most things. I wandered up to the till and placed my shopping on the counter.

"You'll be Jonno then, I'm Stan."

Stan was a tall, thin man with dark hair and skin the colour and texture of a leather wallet. I assumed that he owned the place.

"You know your horse flesh don't you?"

Obviously news travels fast in Rainbow.

I grimaced, "Not really, just beginner's luck."

Stan was referring to my purple streak at last night's video horse racing at the Eureka Hotel. I could vaguely remember the final race ending in a hail of missiles hurled at the TV screen accompanied by a bloke blowing on a bugle - and then a wodge of cash being thrust into my hands.

The store was like a living museum. Its centrepiece was the till, a work of art, silver and magnificently ornate. It was, however, unusual in one respect. Each key had a piece of cardboard stuck to it and each piece of cardboard had a number written in green marker pen. I was intrigued.

The till still registered prices in pounds, a currency which had not been in use in those parts since the sixties. Stan rang in my purchases. My yoghurt which was one dollar thirty-nine came up as seventeen shillings and sixpence ha'penny, shampoo at a dollar ninety-nine rang in at two pounds six and eightpence. The grand total appeared as twenty-seven pounds three shillings and fourpence.

Stan picked up an enormous board about a yard square. It had a complicated grid written on it and the grid was full of numbers.

Stan ran his fingers across, "That will be eight dollars fifty, Jonno," he said.

How does that work, I wondered? but, as Stan seemed as honest as the day was long, I knew that the thought of cheating anybody would have never crossed his mind.

As I paid I noticed that Stan was looking at me in an odd way. He asked me a question I'll never forget.

"How are you fixed for the mongrels?"

Now there's a question. "How are you fixed for the mongrels?" I don't know whether you've ever been asked that. I certainly hadn't, and was at a loss for an answer.

I thought, for a moment, that "the mongrels" might be a local euphemism for some kind of embarrassing infection before I realised that Stan was actually referring to the forthcoming footy game against the old enemy, the aptly named Jeparit Mongrels.

I knew Rainbow was short of players and unless I was careful, I was in danger of being called up, so I swiftly changed the subject.

I mentioned how impressed I was by the till. I was even more impressed when Stan told me it was nearly a hundred years old.

He must've noticed something in my reaction to its age because a faraway look came into his eyes. He took a breath, paused and asked,

"Do you want to buy some braces?"

I didn't, but Stan wasn't taking no for an answer.

He led me out to the back, into a large store room, one side of which was shelved from floor to ceiling. Each shelf was stacked with piles of objects wrapped in yellowing tissue paper. They looked like slabs of bacon. He lifted a package down and handed it to me. I unwrapped it. It contained a pair of cream coloured braces with dark brown leather tabs. Each pair was emblazoned with the legend "AIF – Australian Imperial Forces." They were magnificent but I still didn't want braces.

"You can have these for a dollar" Stan said. "I've got heaps. My grandfather bought them, army surplus, in 1919."

I stared. There must've been at least ten thousand pairs, enough braces to support the Sydney Harbour Bridge.

"How many of these do you sell a week?", I asked.

"Not many. Sold a pair last year but."

I felt rather sorry for Stan and gave him a dollar and walked back out into the sun with my purchases in a small plastic bag.

I headed up Anzac Street towards the bank to open an account. On my way I saw the bugler from the previous evening outside the greengrocer's unloading produce from the back of a large truck. His name was Mario, a hefty man with tufts of what looked like carpet sprouting from inside his singlet.

"G'day Jonno", he called from across the street and waved for me to come over.

"Here, have this for the Missus," and proffered a large marrow.

I explained that I wasn't married.

He grinned.

"Here, take this instead," and handed me a cauliflower.

"You wanna come to Melbourne Thursday night?"

"Can't, I'm teaching on Friday."

"Pull a sickie mate – they all do it. Listen," he said in a lower voice, "you and me, we'll leave here at seven, get to town about midnight. Then we'll go to Moonie Ponds, have a few beers, see some prostitutes, then go to Victoria market, pick up the fruit and veg and come home. You'll like it."

I winced.

Then he whispered, "Do not tell Allegra, she fucking kill me if she find out."

I assumed, correctly, that Allegra was his wife. I also assumed that Mario's 'business trips' to Melbourne were Rainbow's worst kept secret.

"No, sorry, I can't."

"Okay Jonno, you say 'no' now but wait, two, three weeks – you will come – and you get more than a cauliflower." He laughed and patted my back.

As I waited in the queue at the Commonwealth Bank, I wondered what would be worse, turning out in the annual Jeparit grudge match or ending up in a wrestling bout with Mario and some Moonee Ponds prostitutes. The nightmare scenario was that I could end up doing both.

Chapter 10
Four Down

The traffic lights turned red as I pulled across the bridge over the Fitzroy River and, as I waited for them to change, I saw it. It was impossible not to. Painted bright pink and black, "Kings Cash Exchange" was a pawn shop as big as a battleship, housed in what looked as though it had once been a classic Aussie pub. I drew up outside. I was desperate, maybe I could raise a few dollars by selling my camera. I grabbed the Olympus and wandered in.

When I was a teenager I once owned a pair of thick crepe soled shoes that were called "brothel creepers" and the carpet in the pawn shop reminded me of them because the floor was spongy and rather sticky, as if designed to prevent anyone from making a quick getaway. Behind the counter sat a couple, or rather two versions of the same person. Between them they had a combined vocabulary, it seemed, of about fifty words and they regarded me with almost total disinterest, if not contempt. The woman was smoking and filling in answers to a crossword. As I stood there, I found myself reading the clues.

"Four down, 'Thick as -----'"

"Shit" I said. I had meant this to be inaudible but clearly it wasn't.

The man looked up, offended.

It was then I noticed a sign on the wall. "Foul language will not be tolerated," above which was another, "Best prices paid for gold and silver."

"I'll be back in a second" I needn't have said anything, because there was no answer.

I found it tucked away in the glove compartment. The glass bottle with my sample of Wedderburn gold which I had picked up weeks ago. I knew that it was probably worthless, but hey, it was worth a try.

Back inside, I put it on the counter.

"How much for this?"

The woman didn't even glance up. The man shifted his backside, picked up the bottle, unscrewed the top and dropped the nugget into his palm. He then poked at it with a knife. Next, he produced a white tile and scraped the nugget across it. It left a yellow streak. Finally, he reached into a drawer and took out a small dropper from which he deposited a clear liquid onto the nugget.

After a couple of moments, he wheezed, "Selling or pawning?"

"Selling" His taciturn nature was infectious.

He placed the gold on a set of scales. I could see the weight, just under two ounces.

"Five hundred bucks. Take it or leave it."

"What?" I was astonished. I hadn't expected it to be worth anything.

"OK, five seventy-five. Last offer."

I nodded and waited as the cash was counted into my hands.

As I turned to leave, the woman spoke.

"Thieves," she said, "thieves." I thought she was talking about her customers and didn't realise until sometime later that she had, against all the odds, actually solved four down.

Chapter 11
Christmas at the Rum Jungle Hotel

The town centre consisted of about four features, a telephone booth, a grocery store, an enormous gum tree and what looked to me like the world's biggest pub, the Rum Jungle Hotel.

Its foyer was decorated with a limp garland and a plastic Christmas tree which looked long past its sell by date.

Now, I perhaps had better tell you that the term 'hotel' is probably a crime against advertising standards – it did, in fact, have rooms, but its main business was beer.

As I was checking in, however, I noticed something in its favour, a collection of second hand paperbacks for guests to borrow. I was riffling through them when the receptionist, a young woman, asked if I was looking for anything in particular.

"Oh, I don't know, anything, adventure, foreign travel, stuff like that." One book in particular looked appealing, 'Heart of Darkness'. I picked it up and was scanning it when the receptionist said, "I don't think that's quite what you think it is."

"Why not?"

"Well, the guy who left it here said," and she looked around before whispering quietly, "it's all about a bloke who takes a steamer up the Congo, if you know what I mean."

Nevertheless, I took it, as a Christmas present to myself and the key to a room that looked and felt as though it had been made of a combination of wood chip and asbestos fibre. I showered and lay on the bed with my book and, as is my habit, turned to the last page to see how things panned out. It didn't look too much like a fun read as the words which leapt out at me were "The horror, the horror".

Nevertheless, I leafed back to the beginning but only managed a couple of pages before I dozed off.

I woke about half an hour later and went in search of food.

I guess you've heard of Phil Spector's famous 'wall of sound', well, entering the bar, the effect was like someone had turned up all the faders to get full saturation.

It took a couple of moments to recover from the wave of noise and for my eyes to adjust as I stepped into the maelstrom. The place was heaving, with what must have been over a hundred blokes all wearing blue shorts and stained singlets, chugging down beers as though there was no tomorrow, which, judging by their alcohol intake might have been a wise precaution.

The Christmas 'counter tea' was in full swing. Of course, there was no turkey so I opted for the Barramundi which, hereafter, I will refer to as the 'hot water bottle fish', so named because it was deep fried with about an inch of batter on its outside covering an object that looked like a fillet of fish, but which had the taste and consistency of rubber. I was just wondering if what I was eating was injurious to health, when the waitress rolled up.

"Aren't cha eating that?"

I smiled in a way that was meant to say "maybe," as I didn't want to hurt her feelings.

I needn't have bothered, because she barked "Well get a flaming shift on, you mongrel. There's plenty of folks waiting for your plate."

I didn't finish the fish. I might have done had I had a Geiger counter, but the more I looked at it, the more worried I became. Eventually I stood up, walked towards a serving hatch and levered the remains into a large plastic dustbin which was almost overflowing with uneaten food. As my fish slipped off my plate, I remember feeling thankful that that was one meal that I'd never see again. Unfortunately, however, I was mistaken.

I was minding my own business when a bloke joined me at the table. He was carrying a large jug of beer and three glasses.

"I'm Wiry Tony."

"G'day, I'm Jonno."

Tony grinned. "Howdja fancy some action?"

Tony's question put me in a bit of a quandary. Was he asking if I was looking for some action with him? And if so, what sort of action? Just then, out of the corner of my eye, I saw the waitress making her way over to us. Sure enough, she parked herself next to me.

"Hi, I'm Raelene, Tony has something he'd like to share with you."

Wiry Tony leant in towards me.

"Have you ever tried 'two up'?"

I was having a waking nightmare. I didn't know what 'two up' was but it clearly involved me and both of my new chums.

I mentally reeled and things were about to get worse.

Tony put his hand down the front of his shorts. He leant forward, grabbed my arm and said

"Cop a look at this."

I hardly dared look. When I did, I was both surprised and relieved. There on the table was a flat piece of wood about a foot long. Sitting alongside it were two old pennies.

Raelene continued, "This is the kip. Tony runs the two up game. He picks a spinner who chucks the coins into the air and folks bet on the outcome – two heads, two tails or one of each. It's a big thing. It's illegal but out here, especially at Christmas, no one gives a rat's arse at a wedding."

Raelene smiled, and handed me two coins. They looked identical to the ones Tony had. "Just look after these beauties and when Tony tips you the wink you'll be the spinner. All you have to do is the switch and just make sure that when you throw them, the coins spin, otherwise you're screwed.

"What's in it for me?"

"Plenty."

I smiled. I knew that what I was being asked to do was a scam, but I was broke, so even if the worst came to the worst, I couldn't really be much worse off, could I?

The two up game was held in the back yard of the hotel.

About two thirds of the pub were involved. Blokes would tap their heads with piles of cash. These were betting that both coins landed on heads. They quickly paired off with individuals backing tails. The game seemed simple and foolproof.

The spinner was passed from hand to hand, the coins rose and fell, and money was exchanged. I was getting really engrossed when, after about twenty minutes, I got jostled and felt a shove in my back. When I reached into my pockets the two pennies were gone. Almost immediately Wiry Tony shot me a glance.

Time stood still. The kip was pressed into my hand. I wanted to yell to Tony that the scam was off, but I couldn't. As I held the kip, I saw the waitress waving a large number of notes at her head. I was in a bind. I had blown the plan, but I couldn't back out. I flipped the coins, they rose into the air and fell together in the dirt.

"HEADS." A roar went up. Both coins had landed with the king's face uppermost.

I was sweating. Somehow, I had got away with it. But the kip was back in my hand. The waitress now had twice as much cash and was waving it about her head and drawing in more customers.

I flipped the coins again. Time stood still as the coins rose slowly, revolved and fell back to earth.

"HEADS."

Again, two heads were face up. The odds against this were pretty high. The chances of it happening three times in a row were even less. The crowd knew this, and bets were flying in towards the waitress who was tapping her head vigorously.

My hands were sweating as I raised the kip. The coins soared once again, higher than before, and came down together. I couldn't look but I didn't have to, the roar from the crowd told me,

"HEADS."

To one side I could see Raelene moving out of the crowd and then Wiry Tony took the kip from me and handed it on.

Back in the bar, it was unnaturally calm after the mayhem in the back yard. Raelene was looking mighty pleased and, as I ordered a beer, she slipped me something, a thick roll of banknotes, wrapped in a jumbo elastic band.

"Seems like your luck's in, mate." This from an incredibly ugly old timer with one eye. "I don't know how you pulled that one, but you sure had me going."

I shot a puzzled glance.

My new acquaintance smiled and slid something across the bar to me, the two pennies I had lost earlier.

"I lifted these from you before you got the kip. Now tell me, how did you do it?"

I smiled. When in doubt, tell the truth is my rule of thumb. So, without looking up I told it, plain, simple and unvarnished.

"Beginner's luck." I smiled and sculled my beer.

One eye thumped me on the back and, although he laughed, I could tell that he was unhappy with my answer. Nevertheless he yelled to the barman, "Another beer mate, and an extra one for me new chum while you're about it."

Towards the end of the night I bumped into Wiry Tony and Raelene once more. They were in fine form, dancing, for some reason, with a life-sized blow up model of a saltwater crocodile. After that, things got a bit hazy, but I reckon it's fair to say that everything went downhill rapidly from there.

When I awoke I was feeling rather fragile. It took me a moment to get my bearings. I was back in my room but sprawled out by the side of the bed. From somewhere down below I could hear that awful Slade Christmas song booming out across the car park. I staggered into the bathroom and discovered a half empty bottle of something awful called Port of Melbourne sitting by the sink which contained the regurgitated remains of the hot water bottle fish.

I turned on the light and saw a ghastly reflection. My eyes were red and staring and on my neck was a purple bruise that looked like I had either been strangled by an orangutan or bitten by a rabid fruit bat. This injury puzzled me, and I was racking my brain to recall how I had got it. Nevertheless, I forced a smile and was just reassuring myself that this was probably the worst I was gonna feel all day when I heard a noise from the bedroom. I retraced my steps and noticed a shape moving under the sheets.

Who or what could it be?

The awful probability was that it was either Raelene, Wiry Tony or the one eyed bloke. Whoever it was had probably injured my neck.

As I stood there my mind went back to my book.

The horror, the horror.

As quickly and quietly as I could, I grabbed my gear and walked out, closing the door behind me. I never once glanced back.

Chapter 12
Herbie

Herbie was on the run. We might have guessed, but we didn't.

Hilary and I had met him a couple of years earlier on Great Keppel Island. That night the sky was a jewellery box of stars, brighter than any nightscape I had ever seen.

A group of us were sitting in a circle around the fire. The flames, fed by sea salt on the blazing driftwood, burnt crimson, and gum resin constantly popped as embers climbed lazily into the air while all the time, the waves sucked lazily up and down the sandy beach as we began swapping travellers' tales. Rae, a tall, handsome woman was heading off to Borneo, a group of Kiwis were heading south to Melbourne town and, as for the rest, who knew?

"I could do with a beer," this from Brian, one of the Kiwis.

Everyone agreed, it had been a hot day and we were all pretty much hanging. The only problem was that there was only one place on the island that had any alcohol and that was "The Resort", an expensive hotel complex which refused entry to people like us who were camping out at the headland.

"I'll go and get some." This from a guy with short, red-blond hair who spoke with a German accent. I knew his name, Herbie, that he was Swiss and that in a previous life he had been a stockbroker or something. He was young, about twenty-five years old and with striking blue eyes and a winning smile. Everyone took to Herbie.

"What does everyone want?"

We all offered suggestions, knowing that this was just a game of wishful thinking.

"Gin and tonic", "whisky", "vodka" "Castlemaine Four X", it was an impressive list.

Herbie smiled, repeated the order back to us and announced that he would be back in a few minutes. It struck me that Herbie was perhaps serious and that maybe he needed some help.

It was perhaps half a mile to the resort, and I offered to go with him. He smiled and said simply,

"It might be better if I go alone."

Back at the fire the conversation resumed. Nobody expected Herbie to be successful, after all, several of us including me and Hilary had tried to buy drink from the resort but had had no luck. Their 'no sales to non-residents' policy was strictly enforced, and I couldn't imagine anyone getting the management to change their minds. The conversation returned to travel plans and was in full swing by the time I noticed a figure heading up the beach, in the dark, towards us, dragging a large hessian sack. It was Herbie and, as he got closer, I heard a soft, clinking sound. The sack was full of bottles. It seemed that every item that had been requested had been delivered. We all offered to chip in for a share of the drink, but Herbie wouldn't hear of it.

"There's no need. They gave it to me. There's nothing to pay."

His girlfriend, Debbie, gave a little laugh and kissed him on the cheek. It seemed to me that the two of them were sharing some sort of secret.

As we drank, Herbie gave us a bit of his background. He had worked in stocks and shares in Switzerland before giving it all up. The turning point was an incident involving his best friend. This friend had made a fortune trading in Poseidon Nickel, an Aussie company that had a massive boom in the late 60s. The story, as Herbie told it, was that one day, when he came into the office, his friend was standing on his head in the middle of the room stark naked. He had lost everything, including his mind, in a disastrous market crash.

"He left that day and I've never seen him since."

In the months that followed I got to know Herbie and Debbie pretty well. Debbie told us that Herbie had entered the country on a yacht, sailing from South Africa in the company of its owner, the implausibly named Captain Cook. The boat had been almost totalled by a massive freak wave when they were half way across the Indian Ocean. All the power and navigation systems were wrecked, and the boat was holed and taking on water. This would have finished most people, but Captain Cook navigated by the sun using a sextant and targeted a speck of land miles from anywhere while Herbie was hand pumping continuously. This went on for three days and, just when they thought they were done in, they sighted land on the horizon. They limped into harbour and managed to repair the boat. Their adventure, thanks to TV and radio coverage, became a big story and, when they eventually arrived in Fremantle, big crowds came out in force to greet them.

Debbie told me that Herbie had a set of very special skills.

"He has this ability to simply go into places, ask for goods and then just walk out with them. No one ever seems to notice that he hasn't paid. One day I went with him to choose some stereo equipment and the owner of the shop helped Herbie to load it into his car. He even apologised the next day when Herbie went back because the microphone was faulty."

"Things all started going crook when he stole a pair of fifty cent thongs. He got caught and the police searched his flat. Herbie had been on regular shopping expeditions and the local papers said his place was like an Aladdin's cave. He had overstayed his tourist visa and was in danger of being deported so we fled across the border from Western Australia and drove all the way across the Nullarbor to Melbourne. The only problem was that the car we were driving was an old clunker and used almost as much oil as it did petrol, so Herbie had been helping himself to free cans of oil every time we stopped. This would have been okay had it not been for the fact that, just before the South Australian border, he was rumbled. The police were called and searched the car. When they opened the boot they found over a hundred litres of oil. I thought that we were in real trouble, but Herbie turned the situation to his advantage."

Herbie explained that, yes, the garage proprietor had clearly seen him opening cans of oil, had seen him putting oil into his car and had seen him putting full cans into the boot of his car. For sure he hadn't paid for them because they were his cans in the first place.

"Look mate – I bought this lot in Perth. I've got nearly enough to fill an oil tanker, so why would I steal any more?"

The police accepted his story and apologised, and he and Debbie were, for the moment, home free.

Not long after this conversation, a crowd of us spent the weekend at Wilson's Prom on the Southern Ocean, surfing and taking it easy. I was with Debbie doing some grocery shopping when, on our way back to the car, we passed a newsagent. Debbie yelled, "That's Herbie's boat!" Sure enough, the cover of a pulp magazine had a photograph of Captain Cook, his boat and a ripping tale of the freak wave and Herbie's heroics. I guess this simply confirmed what I already thought – that most of Herbie's tall tales were based in reality.

That evening I asked Herbie about his party trick. We needed to stock up with alcohol and Herbie, of course, volunteered. He was reluctant for me to come along but eventually agreed.

"As long as you don't say anything, and you keep quite still, everything will be fine." We waited outside until the bottle shop was empty and then walked in. Herbie, in the lead, was all smiles.

"G'day mate."

"G'day."

"How's it goin'?"

There was maybe half a minute of seemingly meaningless chatter, but during this time, the shopkeeper seemed to enter a trance like state.

Herbie began asking for items and the shopkeeper piled them into strong, brown paper carrier bags. Between some of the purchases Herbie might drop in a couple of words of dialogue, to which the shopkeeper would smile and nod. It was almost as though he had been hypnotised. I noticed that when Herbie made a particular gesture the shop keeper would often do the same. As the last bag was being filled, Herbie shot me a sideways glance. Its meaning was clear. "Keep quiet and don't make a move."

Herbie passed a couple of bags to me and then collected the rest himself.

"Good night," he said.

"Have a good weekend," came the reply. "It's been a real pleasure."

When we were outside in the car park, I asked Herbie.

"What just happened? How did you do that?"

Herbie laughed.

"I'm not sure. Before I go in, I make myself believe that I have already paid for the stuff I'm buying and behave accordingly. Somehow, most people seem to pick up on this and something deep inside tells them that they don't need to ask for payment. They just seem to mirror my behaviour. It doesn't always work, but most times it does. The interesting thing is, the more valuable the stuff, the less likely people are to challenge me."

He laughed. “That’s why I don’t try it anymore for things like flip flops.”

Herbie turned up several times over the next couple of years but by the time he arrived to stay at our house he had split up from Debbie and needed somewhere to crash for a day or two. Three weeks later he was still with us and, as friends were coming to stay, we had to temporarily shift him out of the house and into the shed at the bottom of the garden.

It was at the end of a rather drunken evening that there was an unexpected bang at the door. I figured that it was probably the neighbours complaining about my lurid mural of the Bondi Surf Carnival which I had painted on my bedroom windows, and which was giving no end of offence, and so I wasn’t in a hurry to answer. There was another knock, louder and much more insistent, so I levered myself up from the settee and walked to the door. As I did so, in the hall I passed Herbie, who was carrying blankets and a pillow out towards the garden shed.

I opened the door to discover two burly Commonwealth Police Officers.

“Good evening. Can we speak to Mister Bergdorf?”

“Who?”

“Herbert Bergdorf.”

“I’ve never heard of him.”

But even as these words were leaving my mouth the Swiss Francs were beginning to drop. Of course, Hebert Bergdorf was Herbie.

“We have a warrant for his arrest and a warrant to search the house. We have it on good authority that he is living here.”

Hilary emerged from the bedroom and asked what was going on. The police repeated what they had told me, and Hilary confirmed that we knew no one of that name. Then she looked at me and I could tell that she too had just figured out Herbie's real name.

I think our surprised reaction must have influenced the police because they spent less than five minutes searching the place before apologising. On their way out they told us that the fugitive was wanted for several things but principally for breaking Australia's immigration laws.

As the front door closed, the back door opened and in shuffled Herbie, wearing his undies and scratching his rear end.

"I need to take a leak."

Herbie moved out soon after this and I next got news of him about six months later. A mate of mine, Roger, had had a strange encounter whilst travelling through Queensland.

"You'll never guess who I met."

"Who?"

"Herbie. I bumped into him on a campsite just outside of Noosa Heads. He was in fine form, and we spent a couple of days together. One afternoon we decided to go into town. He said he needed some new board shorts, so we went into a surf shop. I was just mooching around when all hell broke loose. Herbie ran out clad in an entirely new wardrobe and fled down the street chased by a couple of shop assistants and dropping other stolen items of clothing all the way. A police car just happened by and joined in the chase, lights flashing and the siren screaming like bejesus. Herbie was eyeballs out and going at a hell of a lick and got to the end of the street just before they caught up with him."

I know Noosa Heads. The street Herbie was on is a dead end which backs onto a muddy, mangrove filled, estuary.

Roger continued, "Herbie stopped, looked round and took a header straight into the Noosa River. By the time I got there he was in midstream ploughing like a champion for the mangrove swamps."

Roger told us that Herbie had lain in the mangroves until dark, being bitten to pieces by flesh eating mosquitoes, before dragging himself back to the campsite way after midnight.

"Where is he now? "I asked

"Dunno, said he was heading further north looking for work."

None of us heard anything from Herbie for a few years and I often wondered what became of him.

One evening I heard on the news that the Australian Government was offering an amnesty for all illegal immigrants, and I thought about Herbie and wondered whether he would take this once in a lifetime opportunity.

The next item was about a sharp fall in commodity shares and a realisation struck me. It all fitted. Herbie's lack of respect for property, his philosophy of taking what he could, his journey to Australia and that naked man doing a head stand in his office were all connected. I figured that Herbie's "friend" was a fiction, and it was Herbie who had lost everything in that stock market crash all those years ago. Herbie was the man who had disappeared from his home without a trace. He was the one who had experienced the major breakdown.

It's now decades since I last saw him, but rumours emerge from time to time. Everyone's stories agree – up until the point, that is, that he took up the amnesty offer and became an Australian citizen. Thereafter things diverge. Someone apparently met him in Tahiti where he was living as a painter, someone else reckoned he was practising as a marriage celebrant way up north on the Atherton Tableland and, most bizarrely of all, there was a rumour that he had changed his name and had become a specialist in helping people with their immigration issues.

Just a couple of weeks ago, I got a message from a mate down under. A friend of a friend knew Herbie and he had a number for someone who met him not so long ago. So, sometime over the next couple of days I'll pick up the phone, dial the number and wait to hear what's new under the sun.

PART THREE:
THE OVERLAND TRAIL, 1978

I found a living goddess
Well I couldn't ask for more
She told me to relax and so
I headed for the store
Where all the fruits of Eden were on sale
But that was in the good old days
Along the Hippie Trail
Richard Gregory

Chapter 13
If Paradise was Half as Nice

Don't talk about heaven if you've never been to Bali.
Toba Beta

The departure lounge at Darwin airport was heaving, readying itself for the weekly Merpati – Zamrud departure to Denpasar. We had been in Oz for over two years and had been planning our overland trip back home for so long it had seemed at times that the day would never come, but here we were, two intrepid travellers, setting out on an epic journey.

Looking around, what was striking was the age of my fellow passengers – most like me and Hilary were in their twenties and, listening to the snatches of conversation, all seemed to be heading out on the first leg of the fabled overland trail to India and beyond. I didn't know it then but over the next few months I was destined to meet several of them again and again in the most unlikely places.

As I noticed the attendants preparing to call the flight I decided to nip to the toilet, a move which was, in retrospect, most fortunate. As I re-emerged, I noticed three burly officers from the Commonwealth Police questioning two Dutch guys who I knew, Hans and Marcel. Standing to one side was an Aussie with a black eye and a fat lip. I knew immediately what was going on. This was the aftermath of a pub brawl which had taken place a couple of days earlier during which I had given a reasonable impression of Superman as I flew over a wall having been hurled into space by a local bruiser. Carefully, I took my Olympus out of my shoulder bag, captured the scene for posterity and retreated back into the gents' until the coast was clear.

When I re-emerged, the police had gone and most of the passengers had boarded. Marcel, who was at the back of the line, greeted me with a smile.

"They were looking for you, mate. They knew your first name and thought you were on this flight. The guy with the thick lip reckoned that you started a riot at the pub on Saturday and they were hoping to arrest you."

I felt like Richard Kimble in an episode from The Fugitive.

"What did you tell them?"

"Said you'd headed south looking for work. I don't think they believed me. They wanted to check the passenger list for you – but they didn't have a surname and the flight was boarding so they just took a quick look round and left. You're lucky, I guess."

We walked across the runway and up the steps at the rear of the plane. On board there was a wonderful smell of kreteks, those fabulous clove cigarettes that I will forever associate with Bali. Sure, the no smoking signs were on but the stewardesses in their delicately patterned sarongs didn't seem to give a care as they balletted around giving out delicate necklaces of tropical flowers and cold cans of Bintang.

The plane headed north out of Darwin, over the Arafura Sea, clearing the muddy flats of Melville Island as the words of the eponymous explorer came to me

"Farewell Australia, you are a rising child."

The waves sparkled beneath our wings and in the sky towered ice cream cones of cumulus cloud of a size and beauty that you only seem to get in the tropics.

A tray of gado gado arrived – vegetables in peanut sauce – my first taste of this fabled dish. Already I was dazzled by the sights and smells of this adventure and, as we travelled north, the clouds became ever more spectacular, their undersides creaming with the light reflected off the sea below.

As the food was taken away, and just before the fasten seat belts sign came on, I caught my first glimpse of the island – a line of tall volcanic peaks, necklaces of cloud draped around their shoulders - then the aircraft dipped its wing and lowered over a collection of brightly coloured fishing boats beyond which the surf was curling over a coral reef. Then a narrow beach, lined with palm trees, rushed beneath us before we crossed over the apron of the runway.

Over to my left I caught an image of red tiled buildings and a cluster of banana trees, a black and white painted water tower, a tired, dirty orange windsock hanging limp in the tropical air and a couple of ageing fighter aircraft baking in the heat.

Everything seemed strange and exotic, the deep monsoon drains, the red and white painted kerb stones, the grass cropped short and of the most brilliant green, the thick, emerald coloured moss clinging to every wall in the warm dampness, and finally a low, wooden building that looked like a hangar, but which was undoubtedly the arrivals hall.

Because we were seated near the rear of the plane, Hilary and I were among the first to get off. As we walked across the tarmac I recall being bowled over by the sounds, sights and smells of this new country. We embraced Marcel and Hans, laughing as we did so, aware that the dreams of adventure that had been held for so long were now being lived.

As we walked in the damp heat towards the arrivals shed, a thought struck me. I had been at such airports before and knew that there could be a problem changing money. I had a sneaking suspicion that the foreign exchange desk would probably not have much cash and so Hilary agreed to pick up our rucksacks while I went ahead to change some traveller's cheques.

I dashed through the passport control and fronted up at the counter of the bank. I was the first person from the flight to arrive.

The cashier greeted me with a smile and offered me a cup of tea. I thanked her but explained that I just wanted to change some money.

"How much will you change, sir?"

"Sixty pounds, Sterling."

She smiled in an odd way and then handed me a pen whilst I signed the cheques and handed them over.

She examined them carefully and opened a drawer and began removing a wad of notes. She counted them and took out another wad. By the time she had finished I had a huge pile, some forty-two thousand rupiah in total, all red and blue and covered in images of garudas, water buffaloes, paddy fields, and political leaders.

As she counted them out, she asked me a question.

"Excuse me sir, I hope you don't mind me asking?"

"No, go ahead"

"I was wondering, are you a millionaire?"

"No" I smiled, but it dawned on me that in this country I really was wealthy, an impression that was reinforced by the arrival of a blond, long haired Canadian guy at the counter. He also wanted to change money but was told,

"I am sorry sir, we have just run out of cash."

The newcomer's name was Gary. He was travelling with his partner Helen. I told him were taking a bemo to Legian, a small village just north of Kuta. Gary had never heard of Legian but was happy to come along, especially since I was going to pay the fares.

Outside in car park things were progressing quite smoothly. We headed towards a line of small pickup trucks powered by three wheeler mopeds. In seconds we found one going our way. Already there were half a dozen people in the back and, as we levered ourselves in, a middle aged man, all smiles and teeth red from chewing betel nut, came to collect our fares.

I was expecting to pay perhaps six hundred rupiah, about a pound, so was surprised when he said,

"Dua Puluh" and pointed at each of us in turn.

I did a double take. Twenty each, the equivalent of about three pence per person. I knew that petrol in Indonesia was cheap, but this was ridiculous.

I grabbed my wodge and felt a sense of shame as I peeled off a hundred rupiah note and handed it over.

The man smiled and from a fan of notes held between his fingers gave me back a brightly coloured banknote about the size of a bus ticket.

Immediately I did a quick calculation and, judging from the cost of things, realised that I had exchanged more money than I might be able to spend in the month that we planned to spend in Indonesia.

We bounced along pot holed roads alongside paddy fields, in one of which I saw an old woman being trailed by a long line of ducks, whilst in the background, a volcano soared skywards.

After a few minutes we pulled up at a small roundabout where most people got off. I noticed a yin yang sign pointing the way to a restaurant offering special mushroom omelettes and realised that I must be at the fabled "bemo corner" in Kuta.

After a few more passengers climbed aboard we set off again and, in less than a minute, we were out into open country. We were dropped off alongside a narrow dirt path just beyond a small wooden building bearing the sign 'Swiss restaurant'.

Our driver called to us and signalled that we should follow the path.

We walked alongside fields in which water buffalo were grazing and looked out for a place to stay. After about two minutes we saw a painted sign board nailed to a coconut palm:

'Surata 2 Homestay'.

There on a flat, grassy plot stood a single story building with a veranda, sitting underneath which were a couple of Australian women holding court to half a dozen locals who were trying half-heartedly to sell their handicrafts. If truth be told there was much more interest in talking and laughing than in selling anything. They all greeted us with a smile and a cup of tea before the owner, another woman showed us around. Our room was basic – a double bed, a concrete floor and, as there was no electricity, the lighting was provided by oil lamps. The shower, at the back of the house, comprised a bucket hauled from a well. We were informed that there was a constant supply of tea on offer. Just to prove it when we got back to our room, there on the table outside the door was a giant thermos, two glasses, a pile of sugar lumps and a bunch of bananas. Just in case we were having second thoughts, breakfast of black rice pudding and bananas was included in the price which was less than a pound.

We moved in and spent the afternoon on the veranda talking and drinking in the view.

In the evening we walked to the beach to catch the famous sunset and then walked south along the surf line into Kuta.

Poppies Gang was already famous, but nothing really prepared me for it. This narrow street was lined with beautifully ornate restaurants all offering exotic food to the enchanting refrain of gamelan music. We chose a restaurant, the 'Krishna Kubu' and entered. The dining area was in a garden, lit by a myriad of tiny oil lamps hanging from the trunks of banyan and banana trees. I felt that I had entered paradise and wondered what on earth I had done to deserve this. I had a wonderful feeling that things were going to get better and, in the months that followed I realised that I was not wrong.

Chapter 14
The Path of Spirits (1978)

"Orang Asli (lit. 'First people', 'native people', 'original people', or 'aboriginal people' in Malay) are the oldest inhabitants of Peninsular Malaysia."
Wikipedia.

The Cameron Highlands seemed like the perfect place to escape to from the heat of the Malaysian coastal plains. The area was famous for its cool temperatures, rarely more than twenty-five degrees, its tea plantations, colonial architecture and, for the more adventurous, its jungle treks.

We had arrived there on a clapped out bus from Tapah Road in the company of Rod and Fiona, a neat couple from Glasgow. They had both been reading up on the area and the tribespeople, the Orang Asli who inhabited the dense rainforest which surrounded the line of settlements all the way up from Genting, through Ringlet and beyond Tanah Rata.

In no time Rod was sharing his knowledge with us.

"They believe that their spirits are part of the natural world of the forest and that the forest has its own spirits who since the dawn of time have cared for the people who live there. Some tribes believe that they have several souls, most of which you take with you when you die but one of them is freed at the end of life and lives on after death. They also believe that the trees of the forest have souls and, if they hear a tree being cut in the dead of night in the middle of the forest, they are supposed to pretend not to hear it because this is believed to be the guardian spirit of the forest doing something."

We had heard that going for a walk in the rain forest might be a little risky. For a start there was the disappearance of Jim Thompson, which had made world headlines a few years earlier. The American millionaire had wandered off for a jungle walk from Moonlight Cottage in Tanah Rata sometime in 1967 and despite an eleven day search, was never seen again. Some people suggested that he was a US spy and that he had been assassinated, others that he had fallen out with the wrong people in his business dealings, but many others felt that he had simply taken a wrong turn and had got irretrievably lost.

Regularly, so it seemed, people wandered off the track and disappeared, sometimes for days on end, sometimes for good. But we were going to be careful, we weren't going far and so, what could happen to us? There was no way that we were going to get lost. All we had to do was stick to the trail and remember exactly where we took any turn offs. If the worst came to the worst, all we had to do was simply retrace our steps.

In retrospect, our problems started even before we set off. Somehow, we were running late and failed to meet up with Rod and Fiona and so we decided to set off by ourselves. We thought we had plenty of time to climb Gunung Jasar, a jungle peak not more than an hour from town. What we forgot to take on board was the fact that in the tropics night falls very suddenly and if you are out in the jungle things can rapidly go awry. Another issue was our map. It was provided by the local tourist board and owed rather more to imagination than to accuracy. Unfortunately, we didn't realise this until it was too late.

We eventually got to the start of the trail shortly before three o'clock. The skies were filled with fluffy cumulus clouds and the afternoon was pleasantly warm. We made our way with little difficulty enjoying the cool shade of the forest canopy but, as we progressed further, visibility started to deteriorate as a warm damp mist swirled around us. I distinctly remember coming to a meeting of two paths and this junction was shown clearly on our map. It was now about four o'clock but we still we had no concerns about time as we were almost at the summit. But by the time we got to the top the clouds had moved in and we were denied the wonderful views that the peak was famous for.

We sat down, had a drink and then ate a couple of rice cakes which we had brought with us. I tried to take a photograph of Hilary and was surprised to see that there was insufficient light without using a flash. Nevertheless, I put my camera on a slow shutter speed and hoped for the best. I still have the photograph, grainy and blurred as a result of camera shake.

We turned round and headed for home. I figured that we would be back in less than an hour. We were enjoying the exercise and marvelling in the beauty of the forest.

I recall that we came to a crossing of paths. I'm pretty sure that it was the one, that we had seen on the way up but now it looked slightly different. The main thing was that there were not two paths crossing but perhaps half a dozen. On the way up we'd gone straight across at the junction but here there was no 'straight across', rather there were a couple of paths which moved off at a slight tangent to each other. We decided to ignore the advice of the Robert Frost poem and took the way which seemed to be the most travelled. After ten or fifteen minutes this path started to ascend and that told us that we must be on the wrong route. The cloud had closed in even more now and it was getting really gloomy. We turned round and retraced our steps but, within a very few minutes, we came to a meeting of several new paths, none of which seemed familiar. Common sense again told us to follow the largest one, but the problem was that they were pretty much all the same size, and it was hard to choose. After a few more minutes we came to a huge and fantastically shaped fallen tree which we definitely had not seen before. The slight worry that we had both felt now began to increase, especially as the light was beginning to fade. Sunset was maybe only a few minutes away and if we could not find our way out in the light, we knew that we sure as hell would have a great deal more difficulty navigating in the dark. Our plight wasn't improved by the fact that, of course, we didn't have a torch between us.

I took out the map and studied it but without any landmarks and without a compass it wasn't much use. I suggested to Hilary that we just take paths which went downhill, as they must eventually lead us to a stream and the stream would, in time, lead us to a settlement.

As we were about to move off I got a feeling that someone or something was watching us, and then something caught my eye. Time slowed down. It only took a fraction of a second, but it seemed to take an age for me to realise what I had seen.

Alongside the trunk of a tree not three yards from where I stood was a piece of bark shaped like a hand. As I followed the hand upward it merged into a knotty vine that resembled a human arm and, as I followed this upward, the arm became a shoulder and then the shoulder became a head. The owner was looking down at the ground, avoiding my eyes. I was looking at a man. He was almost naked, absolutely motionless and perfectly camouflaged. I also half saw something else. I can't describe what that something was, but somehow, I knew it was a weapon. Perhaps it was a bow or a spear. I'm not sure. I understood instinctively that we must not speak, nor must we disclose the fact that we had seen each other.

I told myself to be calm and was worried that if I made a wrong move, we both might get spooked and something unfortunate might happen.

I spoke carefully to Hilary.

"Keep calm and look this way."

I didn't want her to see the man.

"Whatever you do, don't panic. There is a man standing near us watching. Just try to act naturally." I made a pretence of taking out my camera to take a photograph and, as I did, I cast another glance towards where I had seen him. He had disappeared, silently melting back into the forest from where he came. I knew straight away who he was, a forest dweller and a member of an ancient people who still lived by hunting and gathering.

Hilary and I were pretty shaken up. We were both well out of our comfort zone and by now it was getting darker by the second. Jungle sounds which had earlier sounded warm and welcoming now seemed to hold the promise of a threat. We started off again, moving quickly. We both knew it was important to get back to town before night fully closed in. Nevertheless, Hilary signalled for us to stop again just a few minutes later.

"Can you hear that?" she asked.

I listened and there it was, the distant sound of an electric saw. We took a path that seemed to head towards the source of the sound and, within a few minutes, emerged into a lumberyard in which huge trees were being set about by an enormous buzz saw. Our relief was enormous. I guess that we'd never been more than perhaps a mile and a half from town and yet it felt as though we had been in another world, one for which we were very ill equipped. It also struck me as ironic that what saved us, the sawing of wood, was the very thing that was threatening this beautiful and complex environment.

That evening, as we sat in a local bar with Rod and Fiona, we told them our story.

Rod smiled, pulled out a book from his shoulder bag and opened it at a well- thumbed page.

"You might find this interesting. It's something that the Orang Asli believe," and he began to quote,

"Whenever we lose our way in the forest we are always faced with two paths to choose from - the right path and the path of spirits."

"I think that today, for a while, you were on the path of the spirits."

We stayed in the Highlands for just a couple more days before heading north towards Penang and on to the Thai border. We didn't do any more jungle walks.

I still see news articles about Jim Thompson from time to time but so far, his disappearance remains a mystery.

Chapter 15
Shroom (1978)

"I can see a face coming through the haze, I remember him from those crazy days."
Bellboy, The Who

The sand is fine beneath my feet and the jungle comes right down to the surf. Our place, a collection of half a dozen huts and a clapboard restaurant, is set back aways, just by the end of the track leading back to Phuket town. It's the only place to stay on the beach, but around the headland there are two more, or so I've been told.

We had arrived at midday via a combination of buses and bemos from Krabi.

The air is like warm honey tanged with salt and the sucking sound of the surf is drawing me, so although I've been warned about the rip current, I know just what to do. If it catches me, let it pull me out to sea and, when it loses its grip, swim parallel to the shore for a hundred metres or so and then paddle, making sure that I keep away from the white flecks of foam which show where the current is strongest.

I choose what looks like a safe spot and take the plunge. The swell is regular, smooth and powerful – good enough to practice my body surfing. I've just caught a great wave and am swimming out to meet another, when I see an apparition. A head emerges from beneath the waves, eyes bright red, the sort of red that doesn't come from sea water but rather from about half a kilo of Thai grass. Beneath the eyes is a sunburnt nose and a blonde moustache.

"Fuck me, it's Shroom."

"G'day." Shroom doesn't miss a beat. Even though it's three

months since we met, something in his primordial brain identifies with me, or rather with something I gave him when I last saw him.

On that occasion Shroom had appeared at our losmen in Bali full of magic mushrooms and local grass. I'm not sure why he was there – probably he was visiting Kate and Helen who were in the next hut. Anyway, he was well and truly trolleyed and speaking a language which I believe has yet to be translated. When he arrived, I was rubbing Tiger Balm all over my chest to try and soothe a heat rash. Shroom watched me intently and gave me an odd smile. He seemed particularly interested in the multicoloured design on the jar I was holding. He smiled again, laughed, then reached over, stuck his fingers in and grabbed a great dollop. He was about to eat it when I told him that all you had to do was rub it on your skin. Shroom gave me a crazed smile and began slorming it all over his forehead, cheeks and ears. In two minutes his face was a delicious shade of red – rather like that paint "Cranberry crush" which Dulux made popular a few years later. After a few moments Shroom got to his feet, wandered unsteadily over to a nearby coconut tree and sat beneath it in the lotus position. I'm not sure what other sensory experiences Shroom had undergone that day, but they must have been quite impressive because he was still in what doctors like to call a 'persistent vegetative state' a few hours later when the rest of us walked into Kuta for an evening meal. When we returned, Shroom had somehow managed to shift himself and that was the last time I'd seen him until today.

When we got out of the sea Shroom had some strange and wonderful stories to tell. Apparently, he had followed a similar route to me and Hilary – through Java, Singapore and Malaysia before jumping off, like us, at Krabi and making for the fabled Kata beach on Phuket, arriving a couple of weeks earlier.

First of all though, Shroom was after something, and it didn't take long to get to the point.

"Have you got any of that Tiger Stuff?"

I passed it to him. He took a great gob and smeared it liberally about his face.

Shroom was in a state of grace. He lay on the sand for a few moments before he started to speak. It was odd, something, I guess, like listening to a medium at a séance. The voice seemed to come from far away, possibly because it was fighting to get through a curtain of mushrooms, dope and Tiger Balm. I can't really do justice to his performance, but perhaps the nearest thing to it was that bloke who played the part of Colonel Kurz in 'Apocalypse now'. You know the guy? The one whose words were difficult to understand but were somehow strangely compelling.

"It's up on the beach just beyond the headland."

"What?"

"The boat."

Shroom smiled.

"What boat?"

"The one with all the dope in it."

The story came out slowly. Two enterprising Aussies had apparently purchased a teak hulled yacht somewhere up the coast and had planned to sail it back 'Down Under' where they could sell it for a tidy profit. Just to spice up the deal though, they had packed the hull with about a ton of Thai grass in the form of 'Buddha Sticks'. After casting off, things had sailed along smoothly for about two days until the crew, crazed by the lure of the dope, decided to sample the cargo. Now, I don't know whether you've ever smoked Thai grass, but in those days it was pretty potent; rumour had it that it was laced with opium and that could well be true, but whatever the case, map reading at sea at night whilst under the influence of Thai grass is not a recommended module on any recognised sail training course – but then again perhaps it should be. To cut to the chase, the Aussies suddenly and mysteriously ran out of ocean and the yacht was wrecked just a stone's throw from where we lay.

Shroom opened his shoulder bag. Inside was a plastic bag full of mushrooms and a pile of Thai sticks. I heard the voice of Kurz telling me something. I think it was "They've got about 100,000 of these and they're selling them for a dollar a pop". I was intrigued, so Shroom offered to walk with me to the wreck site. It was slow going. Shroom kept getting distracted and staring at pieces of driftwood and shells and I think we only made it because I'd promised him another blast of Tiger Balm when we got there.

When we arrived, the place was deserted. Sure enough, there was the boat, a beautiful vessel, with highly varnished wooden surfaces and gleaming metalwork. It was perfect, apart from the fact that it was lying on its side with a gaping hole in the prow which was covered in a large tarpaulin. We pulled the shroud back to reveal a mess of wrecked timber, sand and a pile of blue plastic sacks. It didn't require a genius to guess what was in them especially as, almost immediately, a bemo pulled up at the top of the beach and two men ran down and began hauling the cargo away. Shroom hefted one sack to his shoulder and started to move with a speed that surprised me. No longer did he resemble Colonel Kurz but rather that Looney Tunes character, Roadrunner, on steroids. I have to say that if there had been an Olympic event in hauling the dope stash, on that day, Shroom would have been a shoe in.

Back at Shroom's hut, the party was in full swing. Kate and Helen, the Aussie women, had joined us and Hilary had brought along some Mekong whisky. I can't recall many of the details, and it's probably for the best that I don't, but I do have a vague recollection of a python putting in an appearance sometime during the evening and me taking out my Olympus and trying to photograph it. Looking back now I still have several pictures of the floor of the hut and a few blurred images of someone's thumb.

How Hilary and I got back to our hut is a mystery, but I woke with a pain behind my eyes and a strange wailing in my ears, rather like a cat being strangled. I staggered to the sink and poured a glass of water and waited for things to settle down. They didn't. Instead, the wailing got louder and louder, interspersed by crashing and banging, rather like the sound that accompanies Thai boxing matches.

I drew back the curtain and almost shrivelled in the blinding morning light. The sight before me was one that I'll never forget. About forty or fifty villagers, led by a troupe of musicians, were parading Shroom along the beach. He was seated in a chair and garlanded in flowers and had been raised to shoulder height. In his right hand he held a bottle of beer and in his left a palm frond which he was waving to the crowd, some of whom were carrying a variety of objects including a surfboard, a rucksack and a pair of flippers which I later discovered were presents that were to be given to Shroom. Periodically there was a sound like machine gun fire as someone set off firecrackers which just seemed to add to the mayhem.

The procession wound its way slowly to a large fire by the rocks at one end of the beach. By this time a group of westerners had joined the throng, I think they thought they were witnessing some local religious festival. There was a joyous carnival atmosphere. Food and drink were in plentiful supply and Shroom was being feted in a royal manner. A local man told me that Shroom was a hero, and that the village was honouring him. Apparently, he would never have to pay for food or accommodation in Kata again. From what I recall, the celebrations went on all day and for much of the night and it took me quite a while to figure out what had happened.

Shroom supplied the details in the late afternoon, during a lull in proceedings.

"Last night I went for a swim, I was pretty well out of it, and I got caught by the rip. It must have taken me three or four hundred yards out. I wasn't worried, I knew how to get back, so I just lay back looking at the stars. They were amazing. I have no idea how long I was there. After a while I began to hear strange sounds – I thought it was the dope at first, then I was convinced that a whale was trying to talk to me, then I thought I could hear a child crying. It was weird. The crying became louder and then I saw something floating nearby and it was making a noise. I paddled over and discovered a baby. It was just floating and moaning. I thought I was seeing things, but I reached out and grabbed it. For a minute or two I was in a state of disbelief. I mean I was stoned. Above me were the stars. They were reflected in the water and the water was full of luminescence. Every time I moved, my arms and feet left a trail of light. I can't really tell you how I felt. It was unreal. I felt as though I was in a dream. I even tried to force myself to wake up, but I couldn't, so, after a while, I took the baby on my chest and paddled to shore on my back."

At the beach there were about half a dozen people yelling frantically, looking for their lost baby. They had been walking across some rocks in the dark and somehow the mother had slipped, and her child had fallen into the sea. None of them could swim and they were desperate for help. When Shroom staggered ashore they immediately figured that he had heard their cries and had swum to the rescue.

News of the miraculous event travelled fast and in minutes the village was out in force to acclaim its new hero.

The celebrations sparked up again the next day and continued, intermittently, for a while. By this time Shroom was ensconced in the best hut in town and was holding forth, at no expense whatsoever, in the local bar.

Hilary and I left Kata beach a few days later and I've never been back, but I hear that it is now a major resort. We did meet up with Kate and Helen once more, but as for Shroom, I like to think that he found his own little bit of paradise and, perhaps, a never ending supply of Tiger Balm.

Chapter 16
The Atlanta Hotel

I just loved this message which I got a while ago when I booked into the Atlanta Hotel where I had last stayed in 1978.

"Dear Mr Evans,
Welcome back! 1978 is a very long time ago! You will not recognise Bangkok. You will, of course, recognise The Atlanta the moment you walk in. The trees in the garden at The Atlanta are taller, the swimming pool shows its age, but little else has changed. We have refrained from changing anything or 'modernising' because that is how our returning guests like it. We now have third and even fourth generation guests. At least one member of staff is still at The Atlanta who was here when you were here in 1978. 'Anong', who became the restaurant manager several decades ago, started work here in 1973. She is on duty from 15:00 hrs till midnight. Like 'Sam' the pianist in Casablanca, of whom Captain Renault said, 'Rick's wouldn't be Rick's without Sam', 'Anong' is very much part of The Atlanta and is beloved by guests around the world. Tell her you were here in 1978!"

That email took me all the way back to the hot August days in the Atlanta spent swapping traveller's tales. The hotel was one of the legendary places on the overland trail, and like Istanbul's Pudding Shop or the Amir Kebir in Teheran, it was a place to meet with fellow travellers, to exchange the latest news and to read the posts on the notice board in the foyer which might tell you the whereabouts of friends and lovers that you might have met and lost on the road.

One guy, Jeff, a Brit, told us how his bus had been hijacked by bandits in southern Thailand. Another, an Italian named Roberto, was full of tales of fear and loathing from Afghanistan.

The backdrop to all of this was the hotel pool, set in a beautiful garden shaded by coconut palms with a soundscape of late 60s and early 70s rock music coming from a wonderfully ornate Wurlitzer juke box. If all of this sounds luxurious, well, I guess it was, but don't confuse luxury with expense. This was a budget hotel, cheap because, like many others in Bangkok it had expanded to meet the R and R trade of the Vietnam War which had only recently ended. As a consequence, empty hotels abounded and only those offering the keenest prices and best service were surviving. Some parts of the hotel were already beginning to fade, but somehow it was doing so with a certain style. The juke box, for example, only took American coins, dimes and quarters and the restaurant décor was still 1950s fast food chic, like something out of an Edward Hopper painting.

One afternoon, as Jimi Hendrix's Voodoo Chile was booming out, we encountered Paul, a spotty eighteen year old from Nuneaton. He was a trainee cost accountant and had arrived the previous day on a two week holiday.

"I planned to go to the Costa Brava but at the last minute decided to go somewhere else. To be honest I didn't really know where Bangkok was and even now, I'm not altogether sure."

To say that Paul was no oil painting would be a bit of an understatement. He was of medium height, thin as a rake, had a truly awful hairstyle and a face full of pimples. Even though he was in the shallow end of the pool, he looked out of his depth and was grateful to find someone to talk to.

"I'm beginning to wish that I'd gone to Benidorm. I find this place a bit too much. I haven't been out of the hotel yet."

Paul didn't know it but while he was standing there in the water a dangerous predator had him in her sights.

Lounging on chair was a beautiful Thai woman. I had seen her the previous day as she roared up to the hotel on a gleaming brand new BMW motorbike. She was wearing skin tight leathers that she seemed to have been poured into in a way that emphasised every curve and wrinkle. She was, I guess, a dream woman, but one that I figured you might be well advised to steer clear of.

I had already spoken to her, and she told me that she had a rich German boyfriend. He was older, about fifty, he was in love with her, he paid for her flat and regularly bought her little gifts including the BMW. She sometimes visited the Atlanta she said because she liked the people and the music, also she would sometimes sleep with the guests in return for money.

"My name is Chuen Chai, but you call me Chuen."

She called over to Paul,

"Hey, English boy, do you want to buy me a drink?"

"Buy your own, I'm not made of money?"

Chuen laughed, a million dollar laugh, full of white teeth, red lips and full of fun.

"Two Singha beers," she called to a nearby waiter and patted the seat beside her.

"I buy you one, Mr Cheapie Charlie," she laughed.

Paul dragged himself out of the pool and picked up an old rag of a towel and sat down uncomfortably.

Chuen grabbed the towel, rolled it up and flicked him with it, flicked him again and then laughed and threw it into a bin before producing a brand new white cotton one from her bag which she handed to him as she blew him a kiss.

Paul looked uncomfortable and I could see that he was looking for an escape route, but when Chuen accidentally put her hand on his knee as she passed him a beer, his fate was sealed.

When I left half an hour later he was lying face down on a lounger with a look of panic in his eyes as his new friend massaged sun tan lotion into the acne between his shoulder blades.

Hilary and I went up to the north of the country for a couple of weeks and when we returned Paul was still there. He seemed changed, he was tanned, wearing a very loud surf shirt and designer shorts, and sporting a flash watch and an expensive pair of shades. His spots had gone He confidently ordered us a drink. When they arrived he asked for them to be put on his tab. This surprised me. I didn't know anyone else who had a tab at the Atlanta Hotel.

"I've decided not to go back to Nuneaton for a while. My money is lasting very well and, err, Bangkok is really a bit more interesting."

"Have you been out of the hotel yet?" Hilary asked.

"Once or twice - when Chuen had to go to see her German friend, but I'm really happy just hanging around here."

That night the Atlanta was raided by the police. They barged into our room at around three in the morning looking for drugs and didn't find any. Fifteen other guests were not so fortunate. Some were banged up in the hell hole known as the Bangkok Hilton and the rest were given a quick trip to Don Mueang airport and a one way ticket out of the country. After the raid I was a bit freaked, so I undertook a forensic search of our room. I found six separate stashes – all of Thai grass and all hidden in just the sort of place you would expect – under the mattress, on top of the wardrobe, in the toilet cistern and so on. None of the stuff was ours but if any of it had been found we would have been in trouble. I dressed, went outside and dropped the whole lot into a rubbish skip before going back to sleep.

After this, Hilary and I figured that it was time to move on and we were making our plans by the pool the next afternoon when a powerful motorbike roared through the lobby, careered through the garden and slewed to a halt. It was Chuen looking her leather clad finest, her eyes sparkling with rage and her red mouth spitting with anger. Paul was in his usual spot floundering in the shallow end. He waved and smiled and then received the broadside.

"You no good English boy. You give me the clap." The word sounded like "crap" "You been making luff with prostitute from Grace Hotel."

The look on Paul's face told it all. It was true.

While Chuen had been hosting her rich German boyfriend, Paul had been chancing his arm and some other parts of his anatomy in some of the less salubrious parts of Bangkok and some very itchy chickens had come home to roost.

It was clearly time, as the News of the World used to say, for Hilary and I to make our excuses and leave.

When we returned, about half an hour later, Paul and Chuen were friends again, and she was rubbing Ambre Solaire into his torso as "Proud Mary" boomed out from the record machine.

Hilary smiled, "I think they're in love."

I thought so too, and knew that for Paul, life in Nuneaton would never be the same.

Postscript

The Atlanta Hotel was pretty much unchanged when I returned in 2015. Sure, the juke box had gone, but everything else was pretty much the same. I met Anong and we swapped memories of those glory days. My bedroom was identical to the one I had back in 1978, apart, as far as I could tell, from the absence of hidden drugs stashes.

Oh, and by the way, although I looked, I didn't see any motorbikes parked by the pool.

Chapter 17
The Man with the Golden Thing

"No firearms or explosives may be brought into this building without the permission of the manager."
Bank of India, Calcutta.

To say that arriving in India was a culture shock was an understatement.

Dum Dum airport, the gateway to Calcutta, was as hot as the proverbial hobs of hell. Things weren't helped by the fact that all of the ceiling fans were at a standstill.

"It is that damned load shedding" a helpful customs official told me. "The blighters are always doing the load shedding and it is just not cricket."

Somehow, I gathered that load shedding was a quaint term for a power cut.

We made it through the heat to the exit, poured into a taxi and made our way along muddy streets past men pulling rickshaws, heavily laden carts and street side coal vendors who seemed to be living in shacks the size of a cupboard. Every few yards a cow would stroll across roads that were crowded with what looked like half of the people on the planet. All the while the journey was accompanied by the almost constant blaring and blasting of motor horns and, by the time we pulled up at the Red Shield Hostel on Sudder Street, I was wreathed in sweat and feeling quite unwell.

As we arrived a young man dashed out to greet us.

"Good breakfass. Two tose, two banana, jam, tea very good!"

It sounded it, so we moved in.

After a shower and a lie down in our cell like room we ventured out and walked along Chowringhee Road, towards the Tourist Office on Shakespeare Street.

I remember coming to the Oberoi Grand Hotel, in those days perhaps the smartest place in town, and finding a cow jammed in the revolving door. It was at this point that I started noticing things that I guess I had been subconsciously filtering out. Young mothers with starving oedemic babies, children with limbs missing and a man with no legs pulling himself along on a wooden trolley.

I stopped at a kerb and felt a tug on my shirt. I turned around thinking it was Hilary but instead there was a gaunt figure begging, tin in hand, with two red holes in his face instead of eyes.

I swayed dizzily. This was too much. The horror, the poverty, the heat and the noise were too much for me.

"Hilary," I croaked, "I don't think I can take this. Maybe we shouldn't have come here. I have to go back and lie down."

Hilary took my hand and led me back to the hostel.

I had seen poverty and suffering elsewhere, most notably when I had spent time in Sudan, but nothing had prepared me for the shock that was Calcutta.

Hilary was concerned and offered some good advice.

"Just lie down and rest, maybe you'll feel better after a sleep."

I honestly didn't think that I would, and I remember shivering on my bed and wondering how to get away from this place of nightmares before I thankfully fell into a deep, dream filled sleep.

When I awoke, the temperature had fallen by a couple of degrees and, although only a couple of hours had passed, I was beginning to feel much better.

Just off the reception in the hostel was a large lobby area with tables, chairs and settees. It opened onto a wide balcony overlooking the street.

Gradually, as the sun began to set, mountainous dark clouds gathered, presaging the arrival of a spectacular electrical storm which flooded the local streets. At its height there was a massive flash accompanied by a boom of thunder, followed immediately by the entry into the room of an orange turbaned, black bearded Sikh who said in a deep bass voice,

"Is there a god?"

We all burst into laughter and the spell of my culture shock was well and truly broken.

Over the next couple of days we did lots of tourist things – visiting museums, the Victoria monument and getting visas, all the time hampered by the load shedding.

On the way back to the hostel one afternoon, Hilary saw a hand painted poster for the new James Bond film. The legend was in both English and Hindi and the title had both lost and gained a little in translation. I have always liked double entendres and I was particularly taken by the prospect of seeing 'The Man with the Golden Thing'.

Meanwhile, back at the hostel our turbaned friend was keeping us entertained and informed.

"Calcutta is the only place in India where the rickshaws are still pulled by hand. Everywhere else they have cycle rickshaws but here they cannot afford the bicycles."

I felt awkward about hiring a rickshaw. Somehow it felt wrong to be hauled along, using another human being as my own beast of burden.

"It feels embarrassing and demeaning for everyone," I said.

Our friend put me right.

"Sir, there is nothing more demeaning than poverty. These men find dignity through work. You are well off, and it is your duty to help them by giving them employment. If you do not do this, they and their families go hungry. A hungry man with hungry children will care less about dignity that he will about where the next bowl of rice is coming from."

I hadn't thought of it quite like that, and so the next day I took my first rickshaw.

The rain which had started during the thunderstorm was still pouring down, the tail end of a very powerful monsoon. Hilary and I were headed for the Marble Palace but by the time we reached Cotton Street we were soaked to the skin.

Rats which had drowned in the drains floated on the surface of mud filled streets and, as a morass of filth blocked our path, Hilary decided that discretion was the best part of valour and returned to the hostel. I ploughed on into a lively, open air market - porters carrying bananas on their heads, apple sellers hustling at every step, crates of produce sinking into the mud. As I squelched through the market, I took out my camera to take a photograph. I still have the print. In it are about a hundred people. Almost all of them are staring at me. I was the only westerner around and, for the first and only time in India, I felt concerned for my safety. Never before had I realised so clearly just how much wealth I had in comparison with almost everyone else. In seconds I was surrounded by a dense crowd, all wanting to touch my camera.

Through the crowd came a muscular man. He grabbed the camera, looked at it and began singing in English,

"Camera Very, very ni…ce." Then again, only this time louder, "CAMERA VERY, VERY NIIICE." As he sang, he escorted me by the arm through the parting crowd, out of the market, and into a side street.

I tried to thank my rescuer, but he simply pointed at the camera and by gestures asked me to show him how it worked. He looked through the viewfinder and depressed the shutter and smiled broadly as the Olympus gave its satisfying kerchunk sound as the image was taken.

He then handed the camera gently back to me, singing "very niiice."

He motioned for me to take his photograph, a handsome man, a friend in need, standing there in the pouring rain.

A rickshaw driver saw all of this and spoke to me.

"Rickshaw, rickshaw."

I climbed aboard and we wallowed through knee deep water to the Marble Palace. The fare was one rupee and it made me realise just how little these men earned.

Later that day we went to purchase train tickets from an office in BBD Bag Station. The electricity was off as usual and the man selling our tickets told us that the place was "full of lazy blighters who are making the most of the load shedding."

In order to provide the tickets, I had to supply some information. Quite a lot of information, actually. It started off with the usual

"What is your name, what is your date of birth?" and ran through my address and passport details. Then it was

"What is your father's name, what is his date of birth?"

When it got to his contact telephone number, I was feeling rather frustrated.

"Why do you need all of this information?"

Quick as a flash came the reply,

"In case of accident we must inform next of kin."

I thought that the chances of this happening were rather slim, not only on account of the frequent power cuts.

"I think you will find it difficult to contact my father."

"Why is that?"

"Because he is no longer alive."

The man smiled in commiseration before continuing,

"It is merely a formality. What is his profession?"

When we had completed everything, the forms, in triplicate, were placed in a manilla folder and we were given our rail tickets.

I then watched with interest as the folder was rammed between thousands of others onto a shelf that was already sagging under the weight of accumulated documents.

I realised that this process was simply a way of creating work. No one had any interest in streamlining the system because to do so would cost jobs and a lost job meant, hunger, destitution and quite possibly, loss of life. I was slowly but surely beginning to understand this strange and wonderful country.

Our train was due to depart a few days later from Sealdah Station in the heart of one of the poorest parts of one of the poorest cities on the planet. To get there we hailed a rickshaw for the trip across town and over the enormous Howrah Bridge. I had once seen a photograph in the Sunday Times with the caption "This is Calcutta" and it was estimated that there were more than one million people on the bridge when the photograph was taken.

We agreed a price with the rickshaw driver and set off. We knew we were cutting it fine, but our driver assured us we would make it. Unfortunately, after five minutes, Hilary realised that she had left a pair of sandals behind, so we had to double back to get them. As Hilary dashed in to retrieve them, our rickshaw driver seemed stressed. He told me that he thought that we might miss the train and I knew that he thought I might hold him responsible. I tried to put his mind at rest and when Hilary returned, I offered him about five times the normal fare if we made the train.

He set off like an Olympic athlete, barging his way through the streets, and, by the time we got to the Howrah Bridge, we were overtaking everything.

We arrived at the station with minutes to spare. As I paid the driver a gentleman wearing a suit and carrying a brolly saw how much money had changed hands. He started attacking the rickshaw driver, so I stepped in and told him that we had had a deal and we were both happy with it. The man then turned on me and told me that he was a civil servant.

"You have just paid this fellow more money than I earn in a week. This is not right. If everyone does this the civil servants will all be poorer than the rickshaw wallahs. This is not correct."

I really didn't have time to pursue this because Hilary grabbed my arm and pulled me through the crowds towards our platform. There amid the chaos was our train, one of ten thousand that in those days ran every day in India, and there, on the outside of our carriage, was a neat, white sticker with the following details

Saturday 2 September

Second class sleeper: Sealdah to New Jalpaiguri Junction

Berth 23 Mr Jonathan

Berth 24 Mrs Hilary

Time 6.30pm

As we stepped aboard, the whistle blew and right on time we took our leave.

In all the chaos of Calcutta, despite the incessant power cuts, despite the huge scale of the Indian Railways operation, things still worked. Perhaps more importantly, at that time Indian Railways was the world's biggest employer, giving employment, an income and dignity to millions in a country that, at that time, was wracked by crushing poverty.

Sure, things were frustrating, sure there were huge inequalities in wealth, but the place certainly had a powerful pulse that could only impress. As our train gathered speed and darkness fell, I wondered what the future held for this sprawling country and its enormous, tenacious and growing population.

Chapter 18
Wock (1978)

We had met Wock earlier that day by the roadside in Lahore waiting for the Peshawar minibus and had immediately hit it off.

He said that he knew Peshawar like the back of his hand and informed us that Green's Hotel was the place to stay. When we arrived in town late at night, we looked for a taxi as the hotel was some distance away. For some reason, possibly the lateness of the hour, none were available, so we took a horse and cart chauffeured by a very stoned driver. The horse was, shall we say, rather flatulent and this amused our driver no end. His English was limited but he kept spitting and repeating the phrase "greens, greens, good for the heart," and then collapsing in laughter.

When we arrived, and after the air had cleared, Wock announced it was the "wrong" Greens Hotel but that didn't matter because it was full anyway, so we moved into the nearby Khyber Hotel run by the wonderful "International Baba", an ex-British Army quartermaster who promised us that he could supply anything to meet our desires. He was as good as his word because, within ten minutes, despite the prohibition of alcohol sales, he managed to procure three large bottles of Guinness.

He then went on to proudly describe the fact that he had done his best to make the hotel fit for British visitors.

"I have painted each room with special attention to remind you of England." Looking round the lounge I could see what he meant. Hand painted images of Lake Windermere, Scottish highland scenes, an extraordinary rendition of what I gathered was supposed to be Stonehenge and a sensitive study of Dartmoor prison.

When we finally made our way to the bedroom, Hilary turned on the light to reveal that two of the walls were covered by enormous paintings of brown leather armchairs while facing the bed was the piece de resistance, a larger than life painting of a Victorian fireplace. On its mantelpiece was a vase of roses and a cat about the size of a Bengal tiger. I wondered for a moment whether the Guinness had been tampered with, but it had been a long day and we were soon asleep.

The next morning saw us rise at around 6.45 and dash into town to purchase the last three tickets for the Kabul bus, which happened to be a recycled Swiss postal vehicle. As we boarded, I noticed that our fellow passengers formed two distinct groups, about half a dozen westerners on the fabled hippy trail and around thirty or so locals.

We pulled out of town past scrap metal workers, metal fabricators, tented communities, and garish, hand painted hoardings promoting everything from car tyres to shaving cream, each a riot of reds, blues and yellows. The road was a cacophony of heavily laden Bedford trucks, each piled high with cargo, screaming along, belching fumes and incessantly sounding their horns, scattering animals, cyclists and pedestrians in their wake.

What impressed me most about our bus was the number of weapons on board. Every male passenger seemed to possess a rifle, many of which were ornately decorated with silver inlay.

As we climbed the Khyber Pass, the scenery was incredible. Black nomad tents, fortified mud brick houses, abandoned British forts and a streams of luridly painted lorries, decorated with garlands of paper flowers, trundling and blaring their way up and down.

Near the top of the pass, we entered Afghanistan at the border town of Torkham where you could buy most anything you wanted, Persian carpets, Afghan rugs, lapis lazuli, drugs of your choice and a range of locally made Kalashnikovs. I was told, and I believed it, that if you had the cash, and the inclination, you could even end up with your own howitzer.

Wock wanted to buy an Afghan coat and was haggling over something that looked and smelled like a dead sheep when the bus sounded its horn telling everyone to get back on board. Most of the locals had got off at the border and now there were many new faces, several goats, quite a few chickens and more rifles.

As our bus pulled away from the customs post, the interior was a haze of toxic blue smoke, a combination of diesel fumes and Afghan Black. The driver appeared to be on a hasheesh based life support system and pulled incessantly from a tired and well used hubbly bubbly pipe.

I remember pulling into Jalalabad a couple of hours later, after travelling through beautiful desert scenery. It must have been around lunch time. The city has been fought over many times since I was there but, in those days, it was a friendly bustling place with a large main square which hosted an open air market. In the centre of the square was a large wooden dais on top of which was a huge tent like structure, a chaikhana, a traditional teahouse. We entered and as we did so, the hubbub of conversation stilled, a bit like those scenes in westerns where the stranger walks into the saloon. There, seated on plush cushions, were maybe forty or fifty men, there were no women. Each man was wearing loose fitting robes and most wore felt Afghan hats. Everyone, of course, had a rifle.

As soon we took our seats, hot sweet tea was served, and the general hubbub resumed. Several people raised a glass in welcome and smiled and so we relaxed. Our tea glasses were refilled before a large dish of pilau arrived - rice, almonds and raisins with the occasional hunk of goat meat.

After eating we strolled around the market but were dragged away by the sound of the bus starting up and the driver yelling to us to get on board.

Leaving Jalalabad, the road rose steeply, and it seemed like a close run thing as to whether the driver or the straining engine of the bus would pass out first. In the event, as we mounted a final curve we shuddered to a stop above a steep drop, and everyone got out while the engine cooled down. Way below us flowed the Kabul River, lined with poplar trees, while across the valley were range after range of painted hills. The air was so dry and clear that every fold and furrow in the landscape stood out. In the far distance I noticed a small town. Someone told me it was the city of Amber, some seven hours' drive away. I found this difficult to believe because it seemed as though it was within touching distance, but I have since discovered that this was true.

We clattered into Kabul in the late afternoon. The city was awash with red flags and images of President Nur Muhammad Taraki, who was backed by the Soviet Union in yet another chapter in the endless great game of influence between Russia and the West. The atmosphere was febrile, but, for the moment, the western powers were quiet, weighing up the odds and watching which way the political dice would tumble.

Wock knew the city well and led us to the fabled Cable Hogue Hotel. Before we registered he gave us some important advice: "take your shower immediately because it will be the last time you see hot water."

Wock took his own advice, showered and dashed out to a local bazaar. He was a clearly a man in a hurry, a man on a mission.

He returned later that evening looking like Bull Trade, clad in fur trousers, a fur jacket and a Davy Crockett style fur hat. I didn't enquire as to whether he was wearing fur underpants as well but judging from his rather sweaty countenance I think he might have been.

The Cable Hogue Hotel was definitely not the place to be. At three in the morning the police raided the place and a couple of hours later the night manager burst into our room yelling that we had to get up immediately or we would miss our bus. That, I have to admit, was very kind, especially seeing as how we weren't going anywhere.

The icing on a rather unpleasant Cable Hogue cake was the fact that by this time, broadly in line with Wock's prediction, the water supply had completely run out, leaving the toilet looking like something from the film set of Close Encounters of the Third Kind.

Hilary and I moved out that morning to another Green Hotel and our next few days were spent collecting mail, catching up with newspapers at the British Embassy, visiting the local bazaars and drinking Elephant beer.

On our final night we were sitting with Wock in the Mercedes Restaurant near Chicken Street when the Match of the Day theme blared out from the TV. I looked up to see two Buzkashi teams fighting over the corpse of a small cow while an excited commentator informed us that the boys from Mazar-e- Sharif were thrashing their rivals from Bamiyan. When I say thrashing I mean it in several senses. Someone told me that the game is similar to politics and leaders are men who can seize control by means foul and fair and then fight off their rivals. The Buzkashi riders do the same, whipping, gouging and trampling their opponents to gain control of the carcass before carrying it back to their own end of the field to score a point.

Although I had only been in the country a few days I had already been struck by the toughness and pride of the Afghans. They were shrewd traders and ruthless in their dealings. As in Buzkashi, so it was in bartering and politics. Winning was a matter of pride. Anything that could be done to gain an advantage would be done, nothing was off limits. Once you grasped this and reset your moral compass it was okay. If not, you were sure to come a cropper. This is something that most westerners, especially politicians, never seem to have grasped.

More prosaically I was also struck by the fact that Wock was wandering around in what seemed like his own personal fur lined sauna. As we ate, he told me,

"You think it's funny now, but you just wait until the snows come." It was true, winters could be fierce here and there was already snow on the Koh -i- Baba Mountains and change was in the air.

We left Kabul the following day, bidding farewell to Wock as we boarded the overnight bus to Kandahar and Herat. He wandered off in search of deodorant while we were headed for Iran and home.

Like many of the people that I met on the road, I never saw Wock again. Shortly after we left Afghanistan, Nur Muhammad Taraki was murdered, the Soviets invaded, and war came to the country. The hippie trail was broken.

I'm not sure what happened to Wock, but he was nothing if not resourceful and I feel it in my bones that, like me and Hilary, he probably made it out of there just in time.

Chapter 19
The Meshad - Teheran Express (1978)

There's a long distance loneliness rolling out over the desert floor.
Jackson Browne

To say that we were in a hurry to get out was an understatement. The news about Iran wasn't good and we felt it would be a good idea to get across as quickly as possible.

We travelled from Herat towards the Afghan – Iran Border at Taybad where we were warned that, on the Iranian side of the border, guards would go to town in a hunt for illicit substances. This seemed to come as a shock to some of our fellow travellers who had followed the same route we had, entering Afghanistan at Torkham, where its border post was surrounded by hasheesh vendors.

If things were warming up politically in Afghanistan, here things were jumping. A customs official warned us that the situation was delicate before taking us on a tour of a little museum dedicated to people who had been busted, many of whom were still languishing in Teheran's notorious Evin Prison, described in one newspaper as a 'Black hole of evil'.

Our main worry, though, was the ongoing unrest in the country. The Mullahs were mobilising support against the Shah who, in turn, had unleashed the notorious secret police force, Savak, against anyone voicing discontent. This had added fuel to an already unhealthy blaze and once the good old US of A started butting in, things went downhill rapidly. I think it was at the border that Hilary got into a conversation with some people coming the other way.

"Don't stay in Meshad man. It's dangerous. It's full of

fundamentalists. They shot an American traveller there yesterday. Keep your head down and get out of there, fast."

And with that they were gone. The other way.

For perhaps the first time on the journey I felt a sense of apprehension. The only other westerners on our bus were three French travellers and a lone English woman. They seemed relaxed, possibly because they had been up all night chugging the last of their supplies of Mazar-e- Sharif Black.

There were two things I noticed immediately we got underway again. The driver had resorted to standard cigarettes and the road was in fantastic condition – like a newly laid carpet. As we rolled along we slept, only waking as we arrived at the chaos of Meshad bus station about three hours later.

Our French friends clearly had a plan, they were "fatiguee" and were headed for the legendary tourist camp which had standing tents with concrete floors, bunk rooms, a restaurant indeed, everything you could want including a swimming pool. This sounded attractive and Hilary and I were mulling it over when a stranger approached and said,

"Not safe here, American boy shot yesterday." It was at about this time that we lost touch with the English girl in the crowd. She was there one minute, gone the next. We looked for her, but she just disappeared like smoke on the breeze. I just hoped that she had thrown in her lot with the French people.

On the spot we decided to buy a bus ticket to Teheran but when we got to the front of the queue there were none left.

Someone suggested we catch a train but warned us that the last train would depart at 7.30pm and that, because of the unrest, a curfew would begin at eight. Anyone on the street after that would be shot on sight.

By now it was late afternoon, and although the clock was ticking we felt we had plenty of time. Somehow, we managed to find a shared taxi that was headed for the railway station and, as we crawled across the city, we saw tanks at all the major intersections and, on one roundabout near the Imam Reza Mausoleum, a mounted machine gun followed us as we crawled through the dense traffic.

We arrived at the station just after seven. It was eerily quiet. The ticket office was closing, and people were rushing away, in a hurry to be off the streets.

I tried buying student tickets but was told that I would have to pay full price. The only tickets left were in first class and cost 500 reals - about three pounds each. As I started to haggle, I heard the unmistakable sound of a machine gun firing nearby, followed by the crack, crack of a rifle and decided not to argue. I handed over a bundle of notes and the tickets were hurriedly thrust into my hand.

Immediately the shutter fell and seconds later the seller was running across the station concourse, open briefcase in hand, desperate to get away.

There was another burst of gunfire as we dashed out of the ticket hall onto the platform where our train was parked. We found our compartment and lay down on the floor listening to sporadic bursts of shooting and expecting a hail of bullets at any moment. I hoped that these were simply warning shots, urging people to get off the streets, but given what happened later in Teheran, I am not so sure. I began to worry that, because of the curfew, the train might not leave, but on the dot of seven thirty, a whistle blew and we pulled slowly away.

We got up and looked around. The compartment was wonderful, white leather seats and enormous picture windows through which we could see the suburbs of Meshad trundling past as we picked up speed.

We were just congratulating ourselves on our narrow escape when there was a polite knock at the carriage door, and a thirty something year old man with his two teenage sisters entered. The man indicated that they would be sharing the carriage with us and explained that the seats folded down in to one enormous bed and that we would sleep in it together. I was quite surprised at this suggestion, as Iran was socially very conservative, but he explained carefully how it would work. He and I would sleep in the middle, back to back, while the women lay on either side. The Iranian girls thought that this was highly amusing and giggled quietly.

We were tired and hungry, so Hilary and I went in search of the buffet. What we found instead was a restaurant car with white tablecloths, elegant wine glasses and sparkling silverware. We were greeted by the head waiter who addressed us in French and showed us to a table beneath a glittering chandelier. He apologised for the limited menu.

"Je suis désolé monsieur, nous n'avons que la table d'hôte."

We were more than happy – a set three course meal, onion soup, pilau followed by baclava all for less than two pounds.

He then proffered the wine list and of course, being in Iran we chose the Shiraz.

As we ate and drank we felt at peace with the world while the train sped through the darkness.

After eating we were served with an endless supply of coffee and a glass of Grand Marnier to accompany the bill.

Back at our compartment things had been transformed. The bed had been made and our companions were already tucked in beneath an enormous snow white duvet. We undressed quietly so as not to disturb them, got into bed and, lulled by the rhythmic movement and rattle of the train, we were soon fast asleep.

I was woken by light streaming through the window revealing the stark beauty of the Dasht-e Kavir, Iran's famous Desert of Death. Nothing moved and there was so sign of life, not even thorn scrub. The scenery was hypnotic, and I drifted into a daydream of reminiscences of all the things that had happened since I had left home almost three years earlier. Many of those memories were happy but some almost too painful.

Hilary must have caught something in my expression because she shook me.

"Come on, let's find some breakfast."

The dining car was almost empty, and we found a seat by the window and were served grapefruit, scrambled eggs on toast, croissants and orange juice and topped it all off with filter coffee.

By the time we had finished we were approaching Teheran. The scenery had changed, and we were now passing through ever larger townships. We made our way back to the compartment and gathered our gear together as we pulled into the station.

We climbed up a ramp to a large roundabout on Shoosh Street and waited for a local bus to take us to the fabled Amir Kabir Hotel, one of the most celebrated stops on the hippy trail.

Just before the bus arrived about half a dozen Mirage Jets screamed overhead and a few minutes later we heard the crump of ordinance as it rained down on the Hezbollah dominated suburbs in the south of the city.

I looked at Hilary.

"If the Shah is bombing his own people, his time is almost up."

At the Amir Kebir things were rather edgy. People were packing up and leaving and with good reason, because during the events that followed it was attacked by stone throwing revolutionaries. But for the moment the lid was just about being held on things by the armed forces and the secret police. People were being very careful about what they said but fear was in the air.

Some things at the Amir Kebir had not yet changed. There were still large posters of Jim Morrison, Hendrix and Country Joe McDonald and the café still served its famous double egg and chips, the tyre shop by the entrance was still doing a brisk trade but I sensed that this was the beginning of the end of days.

We would have liked to leave immediately but we had done some hard travelling and needed a break.

I recall that one day we visited the US Embassy to see what was going on. If you try to find the place on Google maps today you will find that it has been quaintly renamed the 'US Den of Espionage' and when we arrived, it was surrounded by tens of thousands of people chanting "Death to the Shah" and "Americans out". The place was literally under siege.

At the British Embassy, effigies were being burnt and, while we were watching, a mullah invited us to leave for our own safety. The crowd cleared respectfully as he escorted us to a nearby madrassa and gave us tea and cake. Later he took us on a roof top tour of the building and explained his version of the aims of the revolution and intimated that he was heavily involved. Finally, he asked me for a favour.

"Could you please post this letter for me when you get to Turkey? It is impossible nowadays to send letters out of the country."

I was reluctant, the letter was written in Farsi and addressed to someone in East Germany. I was acutely aware that Savak would not look kindly on me if I was caught with anything suspicious. Nevertheless, I answered,

"Look, I have no idea what this says but if you dictate it to me in English and I can be sure that I will be safe, I will post it for you."

My new friend did just that and the first thing I did when I crossed the border was to buy stamps and put it in the post.

Oddly, I saw this man again, and still see him from time to time on newsreel clips of the day that Ayatollah Khomeini returned to Teheran. He is standing right next to Khomeini as they march through cheering crowds, and I still have no idea what his name is.

Chapter 20
Pierre

It was the arrival of the English nurses that made our minds up. They checked into the Amir Kebir late one night in a state of shock. They had been working in a hospital in Teheran's southern suburbs and, for the past three or four days, had been treating victims of the air strikes which the Shah had rained down from the skies.

We spoke to them over breakfast, and it was clear that things were rapidly getting out of control and that we needed to get away fast.

Just around the corner from the hotel was a small travel agency and together we went to book tickets on the first available Mihan bus travelling non-stop to Istanbul. It would leave at two thirty the next morning.

We spent our last day eating the Amir's famous egg and chips, packing our bags, visiting the museum and updating our travel diaries.

I remember sitting on the bus in the underground terminus half fearing that we might be overtaken by events before the bus left. There were only about a dozen people on board, and all seemed similarly apprehensive. Thankfully, right on time, the engine started, the air conditioning came on, bottles of water and blankets were distributed and, under cover of darkness we crept out of the city like thieves in the night.

Apart from the English nurses whose names I have long forgotten, I have vivid memories of two other passengers, one a Japanese guy who told us that his name was Akihito. Akihito was dressed immaculately in a black suit, white shirt, black tie and highly polished shoes, and sported a pair of jet black Hank Marvin style spectacles, all complemented by state of the art dental work. His luggage was something to behold. It was neat, compact, crafted of high quality leather and had what looked like a myriad of secret compartments.

The other passenger I remember was a French Canadian guy called Pierre. If Akihito was the picture of health and propriety, Pierre was the polar opposite. He looked as though he had been through a very powerful and very unpleasant wringer. He was about six feet tall and as thin as a rake. He had bushy, curly hair and a very unattractive, straggly moustache. He sported a kind of hippy style leather jacket like the one I once saw Dave Crosby wearing at Woodstock - all frills and braids, but this one had definitely seen better days. His trousers were Levis which were pretty much shot to ribbons and his footwear was a very disagreeable looking pair of filthy plimsolls. He didn't have socks. His luggage consisted of a single plastic carrier bag.

As we left the city folks gradually dropped off to sleep but at about five in the morning, just as the sun was limbing the horizon, I was woken from my slumber by a scream.

"My ass is on fire!"

I opened a bleary eye to see Pierre in a state of agitation. He was standing in the aisle of the bus rubbing his rear end in a vigorous and unattractive manner. He saw that I was awake.

"Hey man, do you have some cream for my ass?"

Now this was not the sort of question that I'm asked that often and I guess that my brain was playing for time trying to figure out what he meant by "cream" and why exactly he wanted some for his arse.

"What sort of cream do you want?"

Pierre shot me a glance which was full of contempt. He resumed rubbing his rear with even greater vigour,

"Haemorrhoid cream. My ass is on fire."

By now everyone was awake. I thought Pierre's best bet would be the nurses, but he homed in on Akihito, and with the aid of a deal of shouting, some unusual sign language and repeated use of the A word, managed to get his message across.

At five o clock in the morning on an Iranian bus most people tend to look, shall we say, a little dishevelled but Akihito looked as though he had just stepped out of a gentleman's outfitters.

He stood up calmly, reached for his leather case, unzipped it and opened a side compartment from which he selected a smart toilet bag. From this he carefully removed a pristine, dazzling white tube of cream which he proffered with a small bow.

Pierre grabbed the tube and returned to his seat and then I heard the sound of jeans being unzipped and then the moans of ecstasy as he got to work.

Thankfully it was all over in a minute or so. Pierre stood and zipped up his fly and made his way back to Akihito to return the cream. The tube was unrecognisable. It was bent and buckled and covered in grimy fingerprints and resembled something that you might find on the floor of a garage workshop.

Akihito looked appalled. He gave Pierre a look which seemed to say, "how could you do that?" Nevertheless, he selected an alcohol soaked salve and carefully set about restoring the tube to its previous condition before placing it in its own cellophane bag and packing it away.

After this brief hiatus everyone settled down and I was fully asleep when I was next woken by a yell.

"Calorie faire."

Pierre was yelling again. I had no idea what he wanted.

"My ass is on fire, calorie faire."

Hilary said,

"Do you think we wants a fire extinguisher?"

I wasn't sure, but Pierre was already up and out of his seat and making his way towards the front of the bus.

There then followed some gesticulation. I caught the term 'ass' and 'calorie faire' and a moment later the heater on the bus came on. Pierre looked pleased with himself, wandered back to his seat and within minutes was snoring contentedly.

We pulled up for a drink break somewhere around Zanjan as dawn was breaking. A group of us were huddled round a table in the crisp air as we exchanged stories.

Pierre's was the most interesting.

"I was arrested for trying to smuggle hasheesh," he told us.

"We were getting ready to head back to Canada but were a bit short of money when I hit on the idea of posting a kilo of hash home to raise some readies."

Like all good criminal plans this one was fiendishly simple. They bought the hash, wrapped it in a parcel and took it to the post office where they were promptly arrested.

"The police let my girlfriend go which I thought was really good of them. What I didn't know then was that they were using her to get money.

"They kept promising that if she got cash then I would be released before the trial. She contacted friends back home, I didn't want my parents to know, and she managed to raise a couple of hundred bucks. She paid the money and asked for my release, but the police just laughed.

"I was banged up in a god awful prison outside Kabul. The sort of place you never want to end up. I was put in a cell with about fifty other people. I had to fight for space just to sleep on the floor.

"The deal was, 'if you've got no money you get no food'. Everyone survived on donations from their families and friends or else they worked for the other prisoners, selling themselves or doing jobs for them. I survived because of my girlfriend.

"On my first night inside someone tried to rape me. He made a big mistake because I used to be a boxer, and I gave him a real pasting. Afterwards a Pakistani guy came to me with a knife. 'You have to kill him,' he said, 'because if you don't, he will kill you'. I have to admit that I thought about it for quite a while, but I couldn't bring myself to do it. My Pakistani friend was in jail for murdering his entire family and of course he had nobody to provide food for him, so we struck a deal. He would watch over me while I slept, and I would make sure that he got food. He did this for six months until I got out. It was awful. On my second night I woke up to the sound of screaming and the floor was wet and sticky. Someone had had their throat cut and I realised that, but for fortune, and my new friend, it could have been me. Nine people were killed in that cell during my time there. People were going crazy, literally. It was awful. The only way I could survive was to get stoned every day.

"My girlfriend tried everything to get me out. She visited the governor of the prison who told her that if she could get hold of $10,000 I'd be released. She contacted my parents which upset me, but she got the money. She took it to the prison and gave it to the governor. He took it, put it in a drawer, laughed, and asked 'where is the money? You need to give me $10,000'.

"She told him that she had just given it him, but he laughed again and said, 'I can't see it'. He promised that if she got another $10,000 I would be released. Eventually she came up with the goods but this time it was half up front and half on delivery, and I was set free. I honestly didn't think that I could have survived much longer, and I think that that may have tipped the scales in my favour. The governor probably figured that if I was dead no one would come up with any more cash. I cried my eyes out when I stepped through the prison door, and I was really afraid that either me or my girlfriend were going to be arrested again.

"We were in a hurry to get out, but we didn't have much money. With what little we had left, we managed to get a hundred dollars to my Pakistani friend and bought an air ticket to Canada for my girlfriend. I got a bus ticket out of Afghanistan. I'm hoping to meet up with her in Istanbul."

This was the sort of story you heard quite a bit on the overland trail and on most occasions, you could treat it with a pinch of salt, but somehow this tale rang true.

During the rest of the day Pierre had had to replenish his supplies of haemorrhoid cream several times. Akihito, however had learned his lesson. Now he handed it over like a trained pharmacist, applying a small dab onto a pristine piece of tissue paper. Pierre complained that he needed more but his appeals fell on deaf ears.

Just after dark we reached the Turkish border beneath the slopes of Mount Ararat. I remember the biting cold and the beautiful view of the snow clad peak.

I often felt a touch of apprehension when crossing borders. Customs officers could be arbitrary, whimsical or just plain awkward. The Iranians were brisk, thorough and completely humourless. As we passed over into no man's land, I heard a call from behind me. It was Pierre. He was in a state of agitation.

"They won't let me out. They saw the stamp in my passport from Afghanistan – it says I was caught smuggling hasheesh. They say I have a one month visa and must stay until that expires." Pierre was in tears but before he could continue, he was dragged back into the customs post by two mean looking officers.

On the Turkish side things were completely different. The guards were friendly and made jokes with us. We picked up some items of food, had a coffee and then heard the bus tooting its horn signalling that we were good to go.

We crossed the frozen parking lot and, as we pulled out, I glanced back. There was Pierre sprinting towards us. He burst on to the bus carrying a single red rose and a carton of State Express cigarettes.

"The bastards were playing with me," he explained. "As soon as they thought the bus had gone, they let me go.

"A Turkish guard welcomed me, looked at my passport, and knew immediately what had happened. He took me by the hand into the gift shop and bought me this rose and a carton of cigarettes.

'Run,' he said. 'Your Bus, he is still there. Welcome to Turkey.'" Δ161

The remainder of that night and most of the next day our journey was punctuated by calls for arse cream and demands for calorie faire.

I recall that at one stage we did a huge detour to a remote village to drop off a guy who had just served a long sentence for murder. Our driver explained to us,

"For you this is a few hours' delay. For this man it has been half a lifetime. Please have compassion."

From my initial impressions Turkey was the sort of country I knew that I was going to enjoy.

We arrived at the Pudding Shop, a place later made famous in the film "Midnight Express", in Istanbul at around two in the morning. The weather was icy, and we wasted no time in checking into a cheap hotel next door. Pierre didn't check in. I only later realised that he probably didn't have the money and I feel sorry that I didn't join the dots, but I guess we were all exhausted after forty-eight hours non-stop travelling and not thinking too clearly. He was there with us outside the hotel one minute and gone the next. Just like that. We didn't have his address and of course we never saw him again. But that was the overland trail. Each day was an adventure, each day you would meet remarkable people and each day you would say goodbye to them forever.

For some people, for whatever reason, you just never got time to say those goodbyes. I just hope Pierre's girlfriend was waiting for him as he had hoped.

As we fell into bed, I realised that after three years Hilary and I were back in Europe at the far end of the fabled overland trail and all we had to do now was get some sleep and plan our next steps.

PART FOUR:
MEETINGS WITH REMARKABLE PEOPLE

Chapter 21
Manila Diary 2012

"When I was younger, I became a fighter because I had to survive. I had nothing. I had no one to depend on except myself."
Manny Paquiao

Johnnie

Johnnie, my taxi driver, has painted finger and toenails. They are black and look pretty much like a terminal fungal infection. He is proud of them and wants me to take a photograph.

I ask him why he only paints two fingers on each hand.

"Sir", he replies, "it is no good painting all of your fingernails, unless you are a ladyboy."

So, I ask, "How many fingernails can you paint? How about three on each hand?"

"Yes, is okay."

"How about four?"

"Is okay."

"But not five?"

"No."

"Okay then, what about colours? Can you paint your fingernails blue?"

"Yes, that is good."

"What about red?"

"You are teasing me. That is not possible unless you want to be a ladyboy."

So, there it is. Lots of stuff I never knew about cuticles. Fortunately, the photo of the toes did not come out.

Werner

I don't know whether the St George in downtown Makati actually functions as a proper hotel, but it certainly provides powerful support to the local vice trade. I woke from a night of almost constant interruption from the bedroom next door. At first, I thought I was witness to an attempt on the world record asthma attack but then realised that, if that was the case, then it must have been in the mixed doubles category.

When I dragged myself downstairs to the dining area, a motley assortment of folks were eating breakfast, but my attention was drawn to the bar where a beaming man decked out in an immaculate chef's uniform was enjoying a coffee, and by coffee I mean the real McCoy. This stuff smelled heavenly.

I made my way over and asked where he got it.

"It's my own. Would you like some?"

I nodded, "Yes please."

"I'm Werner, I'm the head chef for the hotel chain."

He told me that he had a sweet job travelling around the Philippines and had lived here since 1969 (they haven't had that spirit here since 1969) and, in a past life, he was sous chef to the Marcos family.

Werner also told me that he has a vast fund of stories from those days and a not inconsiderable number of shoes.

Nestor

Sitting in a cab somewhere near Fort Bonifacio. Nestor, the driver, says the air con is broken. That's a pity because the windows are all broken too – and won't open. It's about three thousand degrees Celsius outside, hot enough to melt lead.

We crawl about half a mile and then the cab comes to a stifling standstill.

"Where are we now?" I ask.

Nestor says, "Global City." I wonder which globe, Mercury perhaps?

Nestor opens the door. It's like a blast furnace. Nestor does this in order to throw up and I reckon I would too if I had any moisture in my mouth.

We sit motionless baking in the heat. I look at my watch. Nestor notices. That's what he does, he notices things like that. He says, "No problem, we will be at your hotel by two o'clock." I'm not sure that reassures me as it is ten past three already and we are still in Global City, and I'm stuck to the car seat which appears to be melting into my back.

Nestor looks ill. He increasingly resembles someone who has been abducted by lobster faced aliens from a very HOT planet and isn't enjoying the experience. I look and feel worse.

Now someone else tries to get in the cab. I'm wondering why not let them share the pleasure of the moment? Then a great cloud of steam emerges from the bonnet. Nestor and I decide to find a bar and kick back for a while and hope that things might cool down.

Inside the bar Manny Pacquiao is holding forth on a jumbo sized TV screen. Manny is perhaps the most famous person in the country, having won a dozen world boxing titles. He is from a poor background and is a mean looking tough guy with a flair for talking politics as well as punching people. Nestor says that he thinks that one day Manny will become El Presidente. If he does, I sure as hell hope he sorts out the traffic in Global City.

Chapter 22
My Week with Hunter S Thompson

Sometime around 1999 I got tangled up in an educational project in southern India. I was helping the Trivandrum Institute of Science and Technology set up some management and technology courses which offered access to honours degrees at the University of Derby.

The idea was simple, study for two years in India and complete the third year in the UK.

It was a win win situation, the students got a cut price degree, the local institute and the university got loads of fee paying students, and I got paid for 'quality assuring' the whole thing.

It was a great idea and things got off to a smooth start. I helped design the programme with an old friend of mine, Mike Cullen, a professor at the university whose academic background happened to be in Pharmacy.

When we arrived, we were picked up from the airport by a guy driving a black Hindustani Ambassador- a car last seen in the UK in the 1960s as a Morris Oxford.

We were taken straight to a city centre hotel, right next to the main railway station. I said I thought we would be more comfortable staying near the beach, but Mike wasn't having it. He seemed happy with his room, especially the fact that it had an office chair and desk and I guess he felt that it was more befitting of his status than a beach hut.

"Maybe you should reserve your judgement until five o' clock tomorrow morning."

"Why do you say that."

"Well, I've got a sneaking feeling that the Bombay Mail is going to come roaring through at some ungodly hour and it won't be a pleasant experience."

Mike laughed this off and, having stowed our gear, we set off to the Institute for our first meeting, still feeling rather jet lagged.

The campus was in an idyllic spot three kilometres away from the famous Kovalam beach and, en route, we caught tantalising glimpses of the surf, the sandy beach and a remarkable red and white striped lighthouse.

We were greeted by the head of the Institute, Dr Nair, and about eight of his colleagues. We drank tea, then a glass of orange squash, followed by some very sweet cakes. The meeting was short on action but heavy on formality. For some reason several of Dr Nair's colleagues insisted on calling me 'Doctor Evans'. I tried to dissuade them.

"No, that's not right. Please call me Jonno."

"Certainly, Doctor Jonno. Thank you."

I gave up and had another sip of orange squash.

By late afternoon Mike and I were keen to bail out before we incurred some serious dental decay.

That evening we wandered the backstreets of Trivandrum in search of toothpaste and mouthwash and turned in early.

At four in the morning I woke with a jolt. My room was shaking, and I was almost blinded by a bright light which seemed to be approaching at a rate of knots. The shaking grew in intensity and reached a crescendo which coincided with the ear splitting sound of a train horn and then a deafening clatter as a long string of railway carriages tore past.

My bedroom door opened. There stood Professor Cullen looking as though he had been electrocuted.

"What was that?" he croaked.

"I did warn you. It was probably the Bombay Mail."

Thereafter at intervals of five or ten minutes there would be repeat performances. Whenever I dozed off, which wasn't often, I felt as though I was having an out of body experience. At one stage I honestly felt that I was living though a re-enactment of the first battle of the Somme.

When we finally emerged for breakfast Mike seemed a lot more interested in my idea of moving to the beach.

We spent all day with Dr Nair and friends, and, at the end of the day, we broached the idea of moving out of the hotel.

Dr Nair seemed a little put out but when I pointed out that we could probably get something quite basic and relatively cheap, he warmed to the idea and even organised an escort for us and so, a few minutes later, Mike, myself, and nine other people piled into two cars and headed for the beach.

We booked into the first place we saw – a collection of perhaps ten small bungalows set in a delightful garden - and arranged to move in the next day.

I suggested that we take a stroll to catch the sunset and we wandered downhill to the sea. As we did, we made a curious picture. Two westerners wearing business suits being followed by a large retinue who walked at a discreet distance behind us. I tried engaging a couple of our entourage in conversation, but they just smiled in an embarrassed sort of way and stood even further back.

Even though it was late afternoon, the heat was intense, so we were attracted to a small beachfront bar from which the sounds of reggae were drifting towards us. Something else was in the air, however, the sweet smell of ganja. As we sat down an American pulling on a large spliff gave us a curious look and I smiled in return.

I ordered beers for our group and eleven ice cold big ones appeared moments later.

As we began to drink, everyone became much more relaxed and, by the time I ordered a second round, everyone was laughing and joking.

As we were finishing our drinks, the American sidled up to the table.

"Hey man, what are you guys doing here, are you making a movie or somethin'?"

At that moment I saw our group as he must have done, watching our odd group trail in line along the beach. We were obviously not casual tourists. One of our group signalled to me. "Doctor Jonno, are you ready?"

Before I could give it a second thought, I responded,

"Yes. That guy over there is Hunter S Thompson and we are making a movie about Kerala grass."

I let this information sink in for a moment before adding "I'm his Attorney. Please don't tell anyone about this and whatever you do don't refer to him as Hunter. If you do he will more than likely give you a pistol whipping. As far as everyone here is concerned, he's Professor Cullen, and he's here evaluating the services offered by local pharmacies, if you get my drift."

American guy seemed delighted with the news.

"Can I speak to him?"

"Sure, but keep it brief."

I got an account of what happened next from Mike as were eating our evening meal.

"What did you think of the American?" he asked.

"He seemed okay, why?"

"I thought he was odd, especially when he winked at me. He said that he knew what we were up to, but our secret was safe with him. But the really interesting thing was, he said he recognised me from my book."

I nearly spilled the beans there and then, both literally and metaphorically, but fortunately, I waited.

"He said it was the best thing on drugs that he'd ever read. You know, it's really strange, apart from colleagues at conferences I've never met anyone who has heard of it and yet I come all the way here, thousands of miles from home and I meet someone like that." Mike paused for a moment, then went on. "What do you think he meant when he said he knew what we are up to? Maybe he knows Dr Nair?"

"I doubt it. He probably just overheard something."

If the going had started to get weird it was about to crank up a little further.

A couple of nights later we were eating in another seafront restaurant when Mike turned to me.

"That couple over there keep staring at us."

I took a sideways glance.

Sure enough, a couple of thirty something travellers had, as they say, 'eyes on' and when they caught my glance they raised their glasses in recognition. This brief exchange seemed to break the ice and a couple of minutes later they sauntered over to our table.

"Professor, err Cullen?"

Mike took off his glasses and looked up, trying to figure out who these people were.

"We really love your books."

Mike seemed astonished.

"What books?"

They laughed.

"You know, the ones about err, em, pharmaceuticals."

Mike couldn't believe it. Here were two more fans. He was even more delighted when the woman asked for his autograph.

Mike was happy to oblige. They proffered the inside page of a well-known and well-thumbed paperback.

Although slightly embarrassed, Mike duly obliged and signed off with a flourish

"Best wishes, Professor Cullen."

The man reached into his bag and I'm sure he was about to pull out a really fat roll up or something worse, but I gave him the sort of look that would stop a Gila monster in its tracks and he took a step back. He opened his mouth as if to say something and I was praying that it wasn't going to be about whether we had a flagon of ether back at the hotel but he said simply,

"When did you first get into drugs?"

Mike leaned back in his chair and smiled.

"I'm not sure. Years ago I got really interested in their therapeutic aspects and how they can help improve our health and well-being." He paused, as if for reflection. "You know, a lot of my contemporaries went into the production and retail sides of the industry but that never really interested me."

"Way to go."

As the couple turned to leave, the man turned and bid farewell.

"Nice to meet you, Professor. Good luck with the project."

Mike gave me a sidelong look as if to say, "What was all that about?" Again, I thought about letting him in on the act but decided to let sleeping dogs lie.

We concluded our work with Dr Nair a few days later and returned home. I went back to Kovalam beach several times over the next few years, but Mike never managed to accompany me. Dr Nair's project eventually got up and running but, as far as I know, the film about Kerala grass has never seen the light of day.

Chapter 23
Sheikh Rassoul and the Necklace of Tutankhamun

Look on my works, ye Mighty, and despair!
Nothing beside remains. Round the decay
Of that colossal wreck, boundless and bare
The lone and level sands stretch far away."
Ozymandias, Percy Bysshe Shelley

I met him some thirty years ago in the Rest House at Medinet Habu, an unglamorous tea stop on the west bank of the Nile near Luxor, a stone's throw from the Valley of the Kings. He was sitting there by himself under a famous photograph of a young boy wearing a fabulous golden necklace inlaid with lapis lazuli.

That morning I had been exploring the ruins of the nearby temple of Pharoah Ramses II, known to the ancient Greeks as Ozymandias. I took a few minutes to sit in the shade and was reading Shelley's famous poem. It talks of the inevitable decline of even the most powerful rulers and that in the end, no matter how great the leader, their temples and monuments eventually return to dust. As I sat there, a man sidled up to me.

"My name is Ahmed. Where are you from?"

"Hi, I'm Jonathan. I'm from England."

"Jonassen, do you want to see secret mummy's tomb?"

"No, not really."

I wasn't really interested, after all there were lots of tombs in the nearby valleys, none of them really secret.

My new acquaintance persisted. He pointed out his house, part of a small village at the edge of the Valley of the Nobles.

"Jonassen, come with me, take tea, eat dates and, if you like, I will show you. It is truly secret."

He flashed a smile.

"If you like it, give me one pound," the word sounded like 'bound'. "If not, pay nothing. Come, what have you got to lose? You will enjoy."

Sure, I had nothing to lose, so I accepted his offer and trekked towards a huddle of low, whitewashed houses a short distance away.

Ahmed's house was like every other building in the village, small and square and very basic. We entered through a wooden door into a small room in the centre of which was a low wooden table sitting on an old carpet. Ahmed moved the table, rolled back the carpet and exposed a trapdoor.

"Wait," he said. He exited the rear of a room through a curtain and came back with two very large heavy duty torches. He checked that they were working, gave one of them to me, and then opened the trapdoor and descended a crudely made wooden ladder.

I followed him down, perhaps fifteen feet. At the foot of the ladder ran a corridor about five feet wide and tall enough to stand upright. By the light of the torches we walked for maybe twenty yards.

Ahmed placed his hand on my shoulder.

"Careful, Jonassen." He led the way across a narrow plank which bridged a deep pit. "It is to stop tomb robbers. Be careful".

Once across the plank the passage ran along to a small room, inside which lay a stone sarcophagus.

"Here is the mummy. Come, look."

Ahmed shone his torch and there lay a desiccated corpse, shrouded in ancient, discoloured linen bandages. Some of the bandages had long since decayed and I could clearly see the nasal cavity, several grinning teeth and tufts of dry hair sprouting from the scalp.

"Take photo."

I took out my trusty Olympus and tried to frame the shot, but Ahmed was in the way. I clumsily tried to explain.

"Please, I want a better picture of his head." I had hoped that Ahmed would step back but something clearly got lost in translation because Ahmed bent over the corpse and began tugging and twisting. I heard a sickening crunch and then Ahmed stood back with the head in his hands and triumphantly offered it to me.

I felt bad on a number of levels, but rather than try to rationalise my feelings I decided it was time to leave. Ahmed put the head back, close to its rightful place, and we retraced our steps.

Back upstairs I paid Ahmed and declined the offer to purchase various artefacts and body parts that he had found. Some of these were no doubt genuine but I really didn't want to be part of the grand old pastime of depleting Egypt's historical treasures.

I made my way back to Medinet Habu with him and we shared a tea. When a tour bus pulled up, Ahmed bid me a hasty adieu and went in search of new clients, and I found myself sitting alone. It was then that I noticed the photograph.

I had seen it before, in a book, and I knew the story of how this young boy, aged twelve, had made the discovery that led Howard Carter to the Tomb of Tutankhamun. As one historian tells it, the dig was about to be given up when the boy, playing with sticks in the sand, suddenly hit a hard surface. He carried on digging and quickly uncovered a stone step. He ran to tell Howard Carter what he had found. The step was the first in a series which led down to the hidden entrance of the tomb. The rest of the story is, as they say, history.

Sitting underneath the photograph was an old man. I approached him and asked if he knew anything about the picture.

He smiled and shook my hand. "I am Sheikh Rassoul, and I am the boy in the photograph."

He gestured for me to take a seat next to him.

The Sheikh said that he remembered perfectly the photograph being taken and the heaviness of the gold necklace of Tutankhamun as it was placed around his neck.

What impressed me about this encounter was the modesty of this man and the fact that so many tourists passed through this place and yet very few seemed to have any knowledge who the man sitting under the portrait really was.

I asked if I could take his photograph. Sheikh Rassoul smiled and nodded his head.

As we talked, I thought about the whole Tutankhamun episode. How Howard Carter had had made the biggest discovery of his and almost anyone else's lifetime thanks partly to a modest young boy who sought only to help and yet whose image achieved fame far beyond his dreams.

My meeting with the Sheikh took place over thirty years ago now and he died in 1997. I know that the Rest House at Medinet Habu still exists but fear that it has probably changed beyond recognition. I have it on good authority, though, that his son now occupies pride of place, seated beneath two photographs of his father. One is of him as a young boy wearing the necklace and the other one has him looking pretty much as he did when I met him.

Chapter 24
Ramayana

The Ramayana is one of the largest ancient epics in world literature. It consists of nearly 24,000 verses .... It belongs to the genre of Itihasa, narratives of past events interspersed with teachings on the goals of human life.
Ramayana, Wikipedia

I didn't want to take a rickshaw ride with Ram, in fact Angie and I told him so about a dozen times.

All we wanted was a quiet walk out of Varanasi into the countryside to get away from the noise and bustle but pretty quickly we realised that we were being followed by a very persistent and annoying rickshaw driver who repeatedly asked if he could take us anywhere. After about half an hour we both began to lose the will to resist.

"Listen," I said, "I promise that when we finish our walk we will take a ride back, but you must stop asking us every two minutes."

"Okay, thank you."

We were as good as our word. On the way back to town he asked,

"Do you wish to see the sunrise on the Ganges? I can take you. Very good rate."

This was something that we had planned to do so we took up the offer.

"Look for me outside at 5.45. My name is Ram."

As we went to bed that night we saw Ram sleeping under the canopy of his rickshaw outside in the street. Even though it was winter, and the temperature was low, he was covered by only a single blanket. He was clearly desperate for our business.

As we left the hotel in darkness the next morning Ram cycled up to us. His face wore a big grin despite the fact that he had two livid bruises. He explained how he had got them.

"The other rickshaw men wanted your fare. They hit me and tried to drive me away, but I refused to leave."

Life was clearly tough for Ram.

The predawn streets were draped with mist and the few sounds of the city were hushed. I heard a cock crowing in the distance and the gently muffled barking of a stray dog. For the most part, the only sound accompanying us was the lick of the rickshaw's rubber tyres on the damp tarmac.

As we rolled downhill, we joined a deserted main road where I saw blanketed figures turning in their sleep in shop doorways.

Further towards the river we entered the lanes behind the burning ghats. Here are the death hotels where Hindus come to die in the belief that dying in Varanasi will release them from the eternal cycle of life, death and reincarnation.

On the shore lay Manikarnika Ghat, where thousands of bodies are cremated on the banks of the Ganges every year, many being released into the river with the hope that their souls may have a direct path to heaven. That morning, in the darkness the perfumed smoke of the sandalwood pyres hung like a shroud.

At this hour there were few customers for the boats. Angie and I clambered aboard one piloted by a young man and we pushed silently out into the river.

The sky in the east was tinged with purple and I got the impression that, on shore, the city was beginning to stretch and wake from its slumber. As the sun rose the buildings alongside the river took on a crimson hue. Already there were pilgrims bathing in its holy waters.

Minutes later the sun was colouring the temples and the facades of the death hotels a warm red, and more boats joined us on the river. To the south, young boys who were encamped along the river bank awoke, began playing and bomb diving from the roof of a half-submerged temple. By now the city was almost fully awake.

We spent about an hour rowing along the shore before returning to the ghats. Ram was waiting for us.

We were hungry and Ram rode with us to a small café. We ordered food and coffee. Ram looked uncomfortable as he sat with us and refused to let us buy him anything.

We spent the next couple of days with him and got to know him a little. He told us that he had a young son and his family lived in a small village ninety miles north of Varanasi. He would visit home every three months or so, which was all he could afford. As he spoke about his village, a weight seemed to lift from his shoulders. Ram had two ambitions, to get a good education for his child and to buy his own rickshaw outright; the one he currently had was on credit at a punishing rate of interest. It didn't seem a lot to ask, but for Ram it was like shooting for the moon.

On our final day in Varanasi the heavens opened. We were starting on our way back to catch our flight to the UK. Ram picked us up and ploughed through the pouring rain to the railway station. We said our goodbyes and then I gave him a gift of money. I wanted him to have his own rickshaw. Ram looked at the cash. They were English notes, but he understood what they meant. As we stood there in the mud he fell to his knees, put his arms round my legs and began kissing my feet. I felt deeply ashamed and embarrassed. I pulled Ram upright. He looked at me and then made a heart-breaking request,

"Mr. Jonathan, will you and Mrs Angela come with me to my

village? Please come and take my son to live with you. I love him and will miss him, but I know that he will have a better life with you in England." He kept repeating this request, over and over, pleading with us to take his little boy.

The three of us were in tears. I explained that we could not do that, that his son needed his mother and father and that they were far better parents than we could possibly be.

Ram was crying and he continued to beg us, but it was impossible.

I took Ram's address and, for a while I sent money to him, but I never got a reply or any idea of whether he ever received it and so, after a while, I stopped. Perhaps I should have gone back to India to find him and his village but within the year Angie and I had a child of our own and then, somehow and to my regret, we lost his address.

As I write this Ram's son will be thirty-four years old. I often wonder about him. I hope that he is having a good life and that, unlike his father, he does not have to literally fight for a living.

Chapter 25
The Heart of Darkness

Mr Angel, our tuk tuk driver, worked on land mine clearance until he became a victim when he lost an eye in an explosion.

He told us a tale when we stopped on a bend in the road just near Swallow Farm, a pepper plantation in beautiful green rolling countryside just a few miles out of Kampot.

"It was just here." He was quiet for a moment. "I was a little child, but I remember the day the Khmer Rouge first came to my village. Everyone was frightened. They gathered all the men and the boys. My older brother was bound and thrown on to an ox cart. The cart stood in the road for a long time in the sun. I knew what was happening and so did my brother. He was being taken away to be murdered."

Mr. Angel was lost in thought and Mr. Angel wasn't the only person with a terrible story.

A couple of days earlier I had been visiting the national museum in Phnom Penh. A woman approached us and asked politely if we needed a guide. I thanked her.

"I'm sorry but I think we'll be okay."

As we were leaving, we fell into conversation. I asked about other places to visit, and I mentioned Tuol Sleng, otherwise known as S21, the infamous prison where people were taken before being carted, literally, to a killing field just outside the city.

I knew from what I had already read that only a very few people, perhaps as few as seven, had ever entered Tuol Sleng as prisoners and emerged to tell the truth.

She told me how to get there, and then, almost as an afterthought, she said,

"I was taken to S21 when I was eleven years old. They questioned me for two days and then let me go." She was quiet for a moment. "My family were all killed."

I apologised for upsetting her by mentioning Tuol Sleng, but she smiled and in a soft voice said,

"No, I must talk. I must tell about these things."

It took us about half an hour to get to Tuol Sleng. It is a former school building surrounded by walls, perhaps ten feet high and topped with coils of barbed wire. Apart from the barbed wire it looks like a normal school building in a normal street.

When I entered, what struck me most were the photographs of the victims. There were literally thousands of them. Many are of young men and women, most of them smiling politely, and it made me wonder if they had any inkling of the fate that was to befall them. I was shaken by this experience, even more so when I had the good fortune to meet two survivors of this awful place. They are there every day, to ensure that this story is not forgotten.

Years earlier I had met a survivor from Theresienstadt concentration camp in the Czech Republic. I had seen him earlier that day at the camp, escorted by a young couple. I learned later that they were his grandchildren. As we waited for a bus we fell into conversation. He told me his story about his time in the camp, the horrors of daily life and his great good fortune not to be transported to Auschwitz in 1944, which meant that by a combination of good luck and good timing he survived.

As we spoke, I felt as though I was intruding on his past, but he smiled.

"It is your duty to ask these questions and it is my duty to answer them."

So it was with the survivors of Tuol Sleng. Their stories had to be told and they insisted that I visit the infamous killing field at Chang Ek where the inmates of Tuol Sleng were beaten to death at night as music and military speeches were broadcast full blast to drown out the sounds of the death agonies.

There is something particularly horrible about Chang Ek. It is not the huge glass case full of human skulls, nor the singing tree where children had their brains smashed but it is the fact that wherever you tread you see in the soil scraps of clothing and fragments of human bone.

And of course, the killing was not confined to Phnom Penh. Everywhere in this beautiful country the people we met had dark stories.

Another tuk tuk driver, Mr. Cho, saw his parents taken away when he was five years old. "I waited for them to return. For twenty years, day after day, I waited and hoped and then I discovered that they were dead, killed in battle against the Vietnamese."

Of course, Mr Cho's experiences are common in Cambodia. Everyone over fifty years old, and I mean everyone, has a similar story to tell and it is not just about the Khmer Rouge.

Dark tourism is a big thing in Cambodia. I have in front of me a business card from another tuk tuk driver from the small town of Battambang. It lists places to see including the bamboo train, the crocodile farm and ancient temples - the standard tourist thing that you would find anywhere in Asia, but it also lists, in a matter of fact way, the killing caves and the killing lake.

Everywhere I went in this country there were places like this. Everywhere I went there were people who had lost mothers, fathers, brothers, sisters, wives and children, and everywhere I went older people were trying to pick up the pieces of their lives.

One day we stood on a hill with Mr Angel and looked out over a valley filled with green paddies and hundreds of circular, water filled ponds sparkling in the sun.

"They are bomb craters. Dropped by the American B52s during the Vietnam war. I don't know why they did this. We were just farmers."

I learned later that the US had dropped nearly three million tons of bombs on Cambodia during the late 1960s and early 70s and displaced nearly one third of the population. Many analysts cite this bombing as one of the driving forces behind the rise of the Khmer Rouge.

I read somewhere that one of the first questions the Khmer Rouge asked of their captives was "Are you an agent of the CIA or the KGB?" Pressure was put upon people to identify friends and relatives who might be in the pay of such organisations and children would be pressured to condemn members of their own family, not that it often helped them. I knew that my friend at the museum must have been asked these questions and I can only guess at the answers that she had to give.

Chapter 26
An Evening with the Mad Strangler

During lockdown I spent rather a lot of time, maybe too much time, on Facebook and the more time I spent the weirder it got. People have been sending me all sorts of odd requests, for example asking for me to post my ten favourite albums or, for some unfathomable reason, pictures with pink in them and stuff like that. A couple of weeks ago loads of people started pestering me to post a picture of a beach, anywhere in the world, no explanation needed. I'm not sure why they were doing this. Now, I've been to a lot of beaches in a lot of places and was idly wondering what, if anything to do, when my brother Richard, who normally doesn't go in for this sort of thing, phoned me up to let me know that he'd posted something.

Now, I have to say that I don't think it was quite what I or the rest of the world had expected. Nor am I sure that like me he quite got the aim of the exercise. Sure, he'd posted a beach photograph, but it was of Omaha Beach on D Day 1944. As far as I know, he hasn't got too many likes so far.

The thought of beaches gave me an idea. And so, the other day I was on the line to my brother Nick in New Zealand. He is hunkered down near a beach in an old school bus that he bought with his Coal Board pension which turned up out of the blue a couple of years ago. Nick used to work down the pit and reckons that the lockdown is a breeze compared to the years he spent underground. He jokes that with the price of crude oil now negative he's sure that one of his neighbours has been syphoning petrol into his bus at night when there's no one looking.

Talking to Nick reminds me of the evening I spent with him and the mad strangler in the fabled town of Maungaturoto about twenty years ago. The mad strangler's real name is Lawrie and he's Nick's brother in law. How he got his name emerged after Lawrie had consumed three bottles of wine before dinner one evening.

"Ah yeah, I miss my Ma. I guess I shouldn't have shot her."

As he is telling me this he is bouncing my four year old son Harry on his knee.

"Was that before you strangled her?" This from Nick.

"Nah, the strangling thing was later, after I'd had one of me turns. The doctors said they're brought on by alcohol."

At this stage I'm watching Lawrie's every move and especially his hands. At that moment I'm reminded of that black and white film, 'The Hands of Orlac', you know the one, where a famous concert pianist loses his hands in a house fire and gets a new pair transplanted from a serial killer called Orlac. In the film the hands have a life of their own and, between tapping out classical piano pieces, take to strangling people left, right and centre. When my mind returns to the present, Lawrie is looking mournfully at his empty wine glass.

Nick plies him with a pint of beer. Lawrie is musing.

"Yeah well that's all behind me now. I'm on the up and I reckon I'm goin' to cut down on me drinking and do one of those Government training scheme things. I'm thinking of becoming an osteopath."

My mind boggles, I have a vision of customers being accidentally throttled to death in the back streets of Maungaturoto and, at that point, decide that it's time for Harry to go to bed and, with some difficulty, pry him free from Lawrie's clutches.

I never saw Lawrie again after that night which I figure is a good thing and as far as I know he didn't become an osteopath, nor did he strangle many other people.

So, as you can see, I'm coping just fine with this lockdown period.

It's putting me in touch with people and memories in a good way and I reckon that if I continue to experiment with social media I might even start to enjoy it even more. That is just so long as folks don't send me any more beach pictures.

POSTSCRIPT

Chapter 27
The Passenger

September 2021

I'm writing this at the last minute. My flight is booked, and the taxi will soon be coming to take us to the airport. Angie keeps asking if I've got everything and, of course I haven't, but I reckon I've got enough to get by.

On the table is a map which a friend was throwing out. It's of Greece. Maps interest me. They conjure up images of places which I've never seen and, as soon as I look at one, I begin to enjoy the journey – even if I never set foot outside the door.

This time though, I really am heading off. Last week I bought us both a one way ticket to the island of Kefalonia and, almost as soon as I did, strange things began to happen. Quite by chance I discovered that an old friend, Rob, is living a boat ride away in the Southern Peloponnese. He reckons he has an olive farm, but I know that is just a front. He is almost certainly engaged in nothing more energetic than wandering down to the local taverna, playing with rosary beads and chewing the fat.

Rob has a shed and says we can lie low there for a couple of days which sounds just fine. I don't reckon we will hole up there for too long before we head south. There are buses to Kalamata and from there to Gythio, where we plan to head to a small island for a while. I've never been to any of these places but already I'm enjoying the trip and it reminds me of something I discovered many years ago and it is this, the trip gives you pleasure in three stages. Firstly, there is the planning where you look at maps, read books, buy your first tickets and explore in your imagination what is to come. The second stage is the trip itself, usually it starts out being similar to the plan but even then, the reality is subtly different. For example, nothing prepares you for your first tropical sunrise except perhaps for Kipling's famous line about the dawn coming up like thunder. The journey, whether it goes well or not, is an adventure and I like adventures. I feel that the less you plan, the better things are. Sure, you might have an end point in mind but, if you are open to suggestion along the way, other pathways always appear, and this is the great joy of travelling.

Then is there the third stage, the period of looking back. This for me is the best part, not least because it lasts a lifetime. Memory though can be an unreliable witness and I often find myself asking, "did that really happen?" That's why in writing this book I have been trawling back through my old travel diaries and photographs and, in most cases, I've found that most of the things about which I've written, happened pretty much as I remembered.

Of course, places are but one aspect of the journey. More important are the people. The people you meet become inextricably entwined with the memory of place and time. Everyone has a story to tell, and I've been lucky enough to have heard quite a few good ones.

Years ago, I read a book by John Steinbeck in which he said something along the lines that we do not take a trip, rather the trip takes us, and we become, in a sense, passengers on that trip. I strongly believe that is true. So now, as I'm looking at the map in front of me, I'm sort of planning to get a local boat around the Greek islands and maybe end up back on Folegandros where I met my friend the diver so many years ago. But hey, who knows, the trip may end up taking me somewhere completely different. In any case I'm sure it will be a blast.

Acknowledgements

Writing this has been a great pleasure, not least because it has put me in touch with lots of old friends. My old Aussie mates Trev and Steph were especially helpful as were my grownup kids, Dan, Jess and Harry.

Hilary, who figures in quite a number of these episodes provided photographic and diary evidence of a number of the stories – especially regarding those related to the overland trail.

My brother Richard who is holed up somewhere on the Isle of Wight read most of these in draft form and helped keep me going by laughing in all the right places. My brothers Nick in New Zealand, Simon in Rio de Janeiro, Adam in Spain and my sister Sue in Kirkby in Ashfield all chipped in with their recollections- especially of the earlier tales.

Many thanks to Adam Crowther and the BBC Radio Bristol Upload programme for playing a number of these stories and to Richard Jones at Tangent Books for his support and encouragement. Also, to my old partner in crime, Chris Loughlan, who helped keep me afloat on numerous occasions, not least in Manila. Thanks as well to Hilary Arundale for her help in editing this collection.

I owe a real debt of gratitude to all these people but particularly to my wife Angie, despite the fact that she says she won't read any of these stories because she's already heard all of them so many times.

Printed in Poland
by Amazon Fulfillment
Poland Sp. z o.o., Wrocław

27200749R00104